Dombóvár

Newcastle Poetry Prize Anthology 2024

Dombóvár
Newcastle Poetry Prize Anthology 2024

Hunter Writers' Centre Inc. and the University of Newcastle
Newcastle NSW 2300

Published by
Hunter Writers' Centre inc.
hunterwriterscentre.org

ISBN-978-0-6453756-6-4

Cover image by Kacper, Adobe Stock
Cover design by Keighley Bradford
Typesetting by Keighley Bradford
2024 Published by Hunter Writers' Centre Inc.

The 2024 Newcastle Poetry Prize Anthology, *Dombóvár,* is produced primarily on Awabakal country, from work created on this and other Aboriginal and Torres Strait Islander lands.

Hunter Writers' Centre pays our respect to elders, past and present, and extends this respect to all Aboriginal and Torres Strait Islander people.

1
stone tulips, all teeth

pretty town of narrow hearts

its sturdy fence

this is not the train but
a train runs through

I remember before myself
there's no one else to

make it a duty now

~ Christopher (Kit) Kelen
Dombóvár
Winner 2024 Newcastle Poetry Prize

Contents

Introduction vii

~ Winner, 2024 Newcastle Poetry Prize ~
Dombóvár 12
Christopher (Kit) Kelen

~ 2nd Place ~
Welcome Swallow 22
Verity Laughton

~ 3rd Place ~
Tornados, and other disasters 23
Jenny Pollak

~ Highly Commended ~
Glass Creek 26
Verity Oswin

~ Highly Commended ~
The Grasscutters 33
Jo Gardiner

~ Harri Jones Prize for a Poet under 36 years~
Lake Days 37
Andrew Menken

~ Hunter Writers' Centre Member Award ~
A Godwit Sonnet Cycle 45
Mark Tredinnick

Aeolian child 49
Jennifer Kornberger

The appeal of paint: A man waits for his execution 56
Sarah Rice

Finials 59
Jennifer Harrison

At sixes and sevens 63
Greg McLaren

Plissken in the City 70
Elena Gomez

The Keeper of the Field 74
Mal McKimmie

Region / Ritual 81
Claire Albrecht

Controlled Burn 83
A. Frances Johnson

boiled potato makes me gag 86
J Marahuyo

The Thought Eagle 89
Jennifer Kornberger

the honey room 96
Jo Gardiner

Night Music Under the Sign of the Platypus 98
Shari Kocher

deadlight blisters write prescriptions in glass 102
Nathan Shepherdson

A Series of Sepia Photos Discovered in the Garage 110
Glenn McPherson

the experience economy 114
David Stavanger

If I hold out my hand 117
Emilie Collyer

Fishbone Ferns 121
B. R. Dionysius

Falling, falling 127
Jo Gardiner

The Luck Dragon 132
Scott-Patrick Mitchell

crechaid 137
Dan Disney

The Literate Detective (Excerpts) 143
Paul Scully

Sonnets with the Moon 148
Damen O'Brien

The snaking accuracy of cow trails 158
Brendan Ryan

A Commotion of Birds 160
Paul Hetherington

Notes on the Dragon year 163
Jane Skelton

Grass Sonnets 16
Jennifer Harrison

Hyaena song 174
Kathryn Lomer

Introduction

Over 800 poems were entered in the 2024 Newcastle Poetry Prize. We read all of these poems blind. It was a demanding task but it also gave us the chance to experience many powerful and original poems. Experiencing these poems convinced us of the importance of the Newcastle Poetry Prize, no other prize in Australia allows for such variety of poetry to be considered in a competition. This is largely a feature of the length permitted—up to 200 lines—however we were struck with how the entries ranged widely in length, from three line haiku to poems filling out every one of the 200 lines. A 200 line maximum allows a poet to be ambitious, to try out forms not possible if the allowance was curtailed.

One of the difficult aspects of choosing winners was the comparison of very different kinds of poems. How to rank a long ambitious poem that may have weaknesses at certain points against a far shorter lyric poem? Or how to compare an intensely personal, emotion-charged poem with a poem that works with history or science and has a more purely intellectual appeal? How to place side-by-side poems speaking urgently of the current day, with poems meandering in the currents of history? We wanted to judge each poem on its own terms and not apply any singular aesthetic too rigorously.

The winning poem, 'Dombovar' by Kit Kelen, ranked very high on both our original lists and grew in stature with successive rereads. 'Dombovar' skilfully integrates thoughtful reflection on important issues, humour, inventiveness and an engaging partly colloquial tone. This evocation of small town rural Hungary carries echoes of the moral ambiguities and violence of settler societies like Australia. Throughout the poem there is the suggestion of a larger, potentially national, narrative, but the reader is left to work through the weave themselves. Sudden transitions between dogs and humans and intertextual asides about fences and neighbours add to the poem's humour. There is also a strong undertone of sadness as the poet subtly creates a self-portrait. With great skill the poem breaks standard idioms and expected word choices to produce a clipped, very tight effect that intensifies the reader's experience. 'Dombovar' uses the form of a poem sequence to powerful effect, shaping a masterful poem that can be read on multiple levels.

The poem we chose in second place, 'Welcome Swallow' by Verity Laughton, is a perfectly crafted short lyric. In its twenty-six lines not a word is wasted. All the dimensions of lyric poetry—sound play, rhythm, shifts in tone, imagery, line breaks—come together to evoke the moment of being fully alive in a small bird. It does this with great brilliance and poise. The suspension created by the repeated 'if …' structure leads the reader onward through image after image till we see the bird with 'this same/ glee of airy volume, this hump and slap of wild/ invisible …' To distil so much intensity and beauty in a traditional lyric form, perhaps a little like Hopkins, is a remarkable achievement.

'Tornados and other disasters' by Jenny Pollak is at once a poem about the difficulties of writing poetry and a beautifully crafted reflection on human mortality. The effort to describe in words the light at midday, the sea in autumn or the shifts in one's moods becomes a reflection on the writer's ageing. Sparsely written and beautifully imagined, the poem offers us the woman 'who resurrects the trees by making them/ her apostles' and summons up the world that exists when we don't see it or when it has truly vanished but continues 'the way that pangolins exist/ and otters on other continents'. Understatement is a strong element in this poem, evoking the experience of losing one's beloved. 'Tornados and other disasters' is outstanding for the originality of its clear short observations and for the way it joins together realms most often kept apart.

The two poems we chose as Highly Commended, 'Glass Creek' by Verity Oswin and 'The Grasscutters' by Jo Gardiner, both skilfully shape their material into memorable poems. 'Glass Creek' brings together the story of a colonial real estate tycoon in Melbourne and the narrator's morning jog by the Yarra, asking us the question 'a colony in the body—how does it feel?' 'The Grasscutters' weaves together intricate descriptions of the natural world with such daily routines as a chat with friends and a swim in the local pool. The poem gives us the beauty of moments intensely perceived as when 'the grass-/ cutters shred long stems of light/ along the road'.

'Lake Days' by Andrew Menken has been awarded the 2024 Harri Jones Memorial Prize. This category was one of the most contested, with many fine poems being submitted by poets 35 and under. What bought us together on 'Lake Days' was firstly its humour and then how it, as a poetic sequence, roamed across forms, stanzas and influences. The ultimate result is a deliberately, delightfully, incomplete portrait of pedestrian town life, by, as the name suggests, a lake, where 'fishes plop' and 'the flies have gotten into the dog food'.

The 2024 Member Prize is awarded to Mark Treddinick's 'A Godwit Sonnet Cycle'. One of many sonnet cycles submitted amongst the 2024 entries, Treddinick's poem uses the form well, interrogating the cyclical nature of tides and human lives. The poem avoids veering into sentimentality or the sublime, while still managing to convey whimsy, humour and love, where the poet concludes that 'Self appears/ To be more like a ragged constellation/ Than a star'.

It was striking how many poems had a rural location. If you relied on this sample of Australian writing as a guide to demographics you would conclude that two thirds of Australians live in the country and only a minority in the cities. In part this reflects the large number of poems concerning the natural world, whether as landscape, plants, trees, animals or birds. There were several poems about floods, which occupied a much larger place in this year's poetic imagination than bushfires.

The present danger of climate catastrophe was reflected in many poems addressing directly changes wrought by global warming, or imbued with a sense of climate grief or dread. Many other poems focussed on other urgent domestic and global issues, many questioned, as Auden famously denied, if a poem could in fact make anything happen. But as readers of these poems, we often felt moved by them, and in the situation of a blind reading we truly were being moved by unnamed strangers.

Many poems focussed on personal stories, often very moving, but in many cases the range of personal details were not well integrated into the poem. The problem of finding an aesthetically satisfying conclusion often escaped the writer, leaving something that seemed less than what a short story or prose autobiography might have achieved. Many of the entries suffered from being recounts of various experiences, whether one's own or another's, whether in teenage years or midlife, that failed to pass through the imaginative distillation required to create a poem. Often the details or personal disclosures evoked a response of 'Why are you telling me this?' rather than building towards a poem. Occasionally poems relating historical stories read like Wikipedia entries with line breaks inserted while many very personal poems felt like rambling conversations that don't reach beyond an implied personal context. That said, there were many strong poems among the entries and only a fraction of these could be included in the Anthology.

It seemed important to us as judges to focus on what the poem achieved, on how successful it was as a poem, regardless of its brevity or length. Tight, well-crafted, shorter imaginative poems to us ranked more highly than longer, overly prose-like pieces that lacked the sharpness or emotional force of the best poetry. In several cases the personal story was all too much like a prose recount with no real music to justify the line breaks and with little daring or originality in language or imagery. A good poem needs to surprise or startle, leading the reader somewhere new rather than remaining within familiar tropes and expected language. It was often a question of finding balance, with many fine musical poems petering out after 150 lines, unable to cohere towards a sense of an ending. And this is what the Newcastle is unique in asking its competitors submitting long poems to do—to be expansive and diversionary, but to return us at the end to enough of a sense of a conclusion to feel sated.

Caitlin Maling and Peter Boyle

Dombóvár

Christopher (Kit) Kelen

Megbűnhődtemár e nép
Amúltat s jövendöt!
—Kölcsey Ferenc

1
stone tulips, all teeth

pretty town of narrow hearts

its sturdy fence

this is not the train but
a train runs through

I remember before myself
there's no one else to

make it a duty now

2
I like to be nowhere—
as far as can be

it's where I'm from, I am

field and breeze, the lean of the land

I don't know them
they don't know me

comfortable to be nobody too

ruins now where they were taken

of course there's a fierceness
could still call belief

must remember for the gone

no one here now has a debt

3
ghost dog, ghost cat—which is why

on brush cutter two stroke day

the id-pack would run, all jaw
best friends, and tear round yappy

all but for the fence, lovely, trained to defend

sit Puli! Hajna stay! drop it!

are simple as children
they like their prey processed

gave me a name and I lost it here

good fences make best dogs most angry

4
all across the Great Plains

on Trabant Saturday, in a diesel puff

our factories shut, heroes abandoned

you go back to look for the good old days

to imagine the coaches,
cauldron and the axe, religion

this is the land of forgive ourselves
for all we've done, will do

5
when one, unseen, goes off in your ear
jump skin

teeth so shine
that really they are barking for each other

a dog for my fence so I'll need one

we could be hounded out with pitchforks
installed as courtiers

a fence to show they know

so loyal, all must bark

6
to see which side they're buttered on
each keeps yard tidily

will always vote for the king, whomever

we were the ones must have run

ever since in disguise

you won't see me, I don't recognize

7
egészségedre—here's your health!

little dance with all paws
then who'll command the tune?

it's how one man makes a whole country

less violins than were

of course the narrowness had to be there

if just once they could go for a walk
they'd be less lonely then

8
'haven't we already suffered?'

and for all the sins we could yet commit

after the rains, there's silt you'd sink in

so much was forest before

now it's happy hour for mosquitoes
they bite through time
hook up with lice and with bedbugs

9
glum cats go
slink, furtive

perhaps they are our silence?

spectres glimpsed in the crossing

or 'here comes conscience'
one might say

10
he doesn't quite invent himself
though would like you to think, a kind of saviour

the gossip breeds
things have gone too far

then the future is like that view you get
from the end of the train when the tracks run away
into the yellow
it was a tunnel then

11
can hear the shouting from next door
some kind of crisis, little seas boil, here's an admiral's cap

sturdy street, all bark as a stranger goes by

see him look down from the top of the tree

defends the bitter loss

says cut down the tree and then you'll be warmer
not mine of course, he means

he gathers in the tithes—ours, yours
for family, for friends across the frontier
so many! and yet these many are few

to speak in a riddle of time

there's a little town in his head
it's becoming a village

12
they sing, who'll see?

some blue, red poppies ragged in weed field

rooster and cuckoo all summer green,
soil quicksand too

here is my father's pet fox

you could walk into the corn just sown

the barking spoils it all

13
if only it were clockwork, could make good then

every hundred years, expelled

these have cultivated a nervous quiet
but you do know they might squeal

have you ever trusted?

lick their young well

scruff them when stiff necked
and some grow alley tough

and some—
if there's cream they'll get it

14
no one's allowed to chase a car

some have eaten through the wire
to take down a bicycle too

15
soon we'll burn witches again

we'll be savage, we'll have just arrived

this one blows with, knows his market

16
lest bite the hand that feeds

the good must accept their fate, face fact

jump Viktor, down Otto, Vlodomir beg

think paper, slipper, pipe, smell fear

haul to the park and home!

17
one may shit on one's own lawn
lay the bottles where you will
that's just superstition

obedient to the old borders
though worshipful, still real

down Árpád, roll over Attila

we know who is who

18
a whistlestop name too long, too fast

water birds, ivy up walls
rye stubble, hills to roll away

the village clouds, and the church run still

so many chimney whispers

19
who ever deserved a country ?

when the paint shines, here's realm was
the buried cross bent top of the crown

20
a little gargle in the morning
throats sore from so much

some have held high office
I think in the case of Caligula
or that might have been a horse

who else can have erected these fences?

21
hold court from a kennel

come out to bark

but they can be bribed with biscuits
will each leap for a treat

22
one kingdom just against all comers

here where the Romans camped

one size fits all there is to revenge

tails wag as I get around
we're nowhere   who'll notice? who could care?

I lean over the gate, blade sharp as their bite
I slit their barking throats

23
meadows and the summer shade
insects known by name

it's better to leave no tracks at all

to be small in a small place no one remembers

to be as good as gone

Welcome Swallow

Verity Laughton

If in the wind the swallow the child
swallow—fat-fluffed, infant-frail,
transparent, light-veined beak agape
to absence of parents of sleek and
swift and startling return—

If in the wind the swallow plants two
twig-like claws on the bold wood of
the balcony and opens to chance or
to ill fortune her thumbprint of a body—
her chestnut breast and cap, dark wings,
abbreviated tail and pale ivory down of
lower trunk that in mammal would be a
belly but in a bird?

'Belly' is too carnal
a word for a bird though birds eat bodies
too of course and her brave little body
strives for balance in the titanic wind,
juddering on the beam, beak tasting
the air as if sipping the sharp sting of the sea.

If she fast-grips—if the black wings flick for poise,
beak bows, head holds, and frail torso twists—
if in time-now this hard mouth of breath is
bird-child's bitter threat, in time-come this same
glee of airy volume, this hump and slap of wild
invisible may be her gift her grit her north
star her tune her tone her small brief bright to be.

Tornados, and other disasters

Jenny Pollak

It's the brightness which stares back at me, and not the poetic ocean.
How it promises to be mine.
How every single time I believe it.

Maybe the light at midday is too general;
the sea in autumn

too still. That even my mood is
indeterminate.

Maybe—and this is how I think it must happen
as you grow older—

it's like the slow fading of the family
in the photographs of the books.

A kind of transparency that refuses
even its own shadow.

How a scream might be preferable.

I am the woman who watches the leaf pirouetting
over the sand and hears singing.

Who resurrects the trees by making them
her apostles.

It's hard to imagine what anyone was thinking
after all the trees came down and it went quiet.

It could be I'm the man in Bly's poem who thinks
Russian wedding blouses will take the place of angels.

Me, with the black spots on my heart
the Presbyterian minister told me

I had. And said that god had put them there.
One for each lie.

A small child with butterflies on her mind.

Now I find it easier to believe in flowers,
who give continually to bees,

than a god who makes that happen
to a child.

The ferry disappears behind the headland
and I see it the way you see things when you can't see them
but you know that they're there.

Like the amethyst my lover gave me. Which I lost when I lay down
on a bench in a park. Somewhere,
when he was still living. Which I imagine

on someone else's neck, in some other city or town.
Just not where I am.

It's how I imagine the world as it exists behind the headland.
But only as my mind can grasp it for a minute.

The way that pangolins exist.
And otters on other continents.

And the molten core of the earth. And many places

I have, and haven't been.

It's how I imagine my beloved exists.
(Just not where I am.)

As the Amazons exist.

And the butterfly on the equator—

the one that's flapping its wings,
who's been blamed for more than it knows.

Tornados,

and other disasters.

Behind the dune is the silence of what a small depression
and a forest of casuarinas can do with the ocean.

I find it more and more difficult to remember the specifics.

The trees are the burial ground for many things.

Today, what began with six chicken thighs simmering
into a clear broth, must end with the chickens,

who breathed the same air
we all breathe: a band of oxygen so narrow

you can walk to the edge of it in an hour
and arrive at nothing.

[1] Lines 21 and 22 reference Robert Bly's poem, *The Waltz.*

Glass Creek

Verity Oswin

young city sprung up on an alluvial plain
teetering on a drowned coastline—they say that when the baby takes inside
you feel a quickening
a colony in the body—how does it feel?

I run the memory mist at dawn
find fleet passage through the
doubt of cloud lingering low
in the crease between the houses
the fog betrays the ghost of a creek
last vein of remnant condensation
mum beneath walking tracks and soccer fields
dry creek—cradle with no baby
I run in deep shoals of grass in the glisten itself
in the quickening

my feet compose long ambulating sentences
at Burke Rd run-on-the-spot
cars are—my punctuation
none of the people inside
the glass
        alive
        while I—running woman
feel the engine of morning throb in my ribs
        while I—running woman
feel the torque of the Earth move beneath

I drink my half words—gulp syllable
a hill, a rise, the gully
the creek slips through the pinch of the hourglass
dew—I write with my feet
with that sweet clear ink from the well of the night

I run I write slowly deliberately
as if untangling myself from a net
follow a thread only to find
a knot I cannot undo—turn back
ghost creek—I did not find you—you found me

ghost creek

I learnt your tinkling name after the fact
        —Mr Hugh Glass, land speculator
        man who sold electric and liquid things
his character also the subject of
great and later speculation
        1862—richest man in New South Wales
        financier, racketeer—imprisoned for the use of dummy selectors
        Gogol and his souls had nothing on this his
crystalline chicanery
        his strawman biz-ness

grand-cestors landed where Glass Creek
flows into the Yarra—landed ever since
        auctioneer debonair down on the banks with Mr Glass
        decent crowd of the rabbit gentry
I admire the auctioneer's blue lizard tongue
        his heft and swagger
        his natty little hammer
glass man—a creek in his name—my ancestors in mine
        under a flag milky with stars
sold the ancestor men this glassy farm

landed

sitting
        pretty

my family
my hokey
        hobby horse genealogy
planted pear trees
on the banks of the beginning
milked their cows
reared their children on Hay's—last paddock in Melbourne
'former farm pasture for sports and BBQs' 'Off leash area for dogs'

grand-cestor listed as 'founder' on Wikipedia
founding—cross between finding something
and its wholesale and deliberate fabrication
        founder—disease of the spring
in which the horse is tended in
        too lush a pasture
        too good a paddock
coffin bone in the hoof gives up the ghost
as much a sign of master's moral decay as of horse itself
founder—here in the colony it is the fallow afternoon

disease of the spring

I follow the rumour of water through designated green space
for the unapologetic cultivation of leisure
man pushes antique pram across ovals (no baby) paints chalk lines on the grass
white stripes peppermint humbugs—sugar drops of empire
Queen Victoria rolled the lozenges round her tongue
playgrounds—but I never see any
children are a disease of the spring and here at the clubrooms
old cricketers superannuated but still rapacious for date loaf and buttered scones
the tea is weak, the ribbon sandwiches threaten to unfurl
outside on the verandah limp in the mawkish light—a flag dirty with stars

dirty with stars

provenance—I've traced the art on this map
back to the titles office
the old masters hang side by side on the floor
the paintings face down
hands above their heads
buyer beware (I cannot see their eyes)
1845—Lots 52 and 53
179 acres (accomplished examples)
"purchased" from the Queen of England
grand-cestral seat of tin pot estate

wattle buttered
so thick on the bread
grand-cestor could hardly build his fences hardly
stake his claim
for yellow
colony gained purchase
with the swing saw with the nasty art of a treaty
and with the apocalypse well under way
in full bloom, in full swing
painted in cows over the people (buyer beware)

purchase

I run in the first person
fall in love with the loop—with repeat play
always run in the same direction
decant electric liquid
quickening of words aloud into my phone
my field notes run off the screen
off the glass page
in baby rivulets
silver diary
of creeks and rivers

I run in
the present tense and in the now
find in
perpetual motion
a kind of flattening of time
find the past
not to be
behind
but all
around

field notes

where the creek flows into Birrarung they built the homestead
white timber painted lady—broad brim verandah
squat and prim on green hillside
homestead has a wife inside—Mary
inside the wife a quickening
many quickenings—feather bed of ancestor children
garlands on their heads at the centenary picnic
Queen Victoria 'had a penchant for floral motifs'
roses on her diadem—I would that the creek would fill again
did they rinse the cream out of the pails on its banks? did the water run with milk?

these yam daisy chains of indefeasibility
we wear them on our heads
spear grass, kangaroo grass plaited together
the young queen beguiles in her wattle tiara
skeleton of a delta
of a wetland
across the chart of days
the tributaries and streams
we built the city on a pane of glass
the houses slide all around

wetland

ghost of a wetland
    if before the marshes were soft with other footfalls
    if other skin pressed the soil
when they open the weirs
the waters washed away the tracks
the skin of the earth is still warm
        bark canoe many canoes
        ply the waters
I hear the wood sing
underwater the plash and whimper of the blade

        canoes empty
cradles without babies
        drift downstream through the city
        tailspin over Dights' Falls
those husks of boats
break up on the rocks
        float out to sea but nobody there to see
to trace the metrics of their displacement
(in my field notes many errors and omissions
in the diary of the body, many excisions)

excisions

now the farm knee deep in private schools
amenity grows right up past the fences in the garden suburbs
my words and days enjambing out of their boxes
    trips and breaks in the circuit—interrupt, disrupt
I stutter when I try to say the word
    perpetuity
I hanker for a tag to tie on the slick
    complicity of

cells dividing, multiplying—the planets in their orbit run around the perimeter
we the spin offs—the poor imitations of a founder

the planets breed like rabbits
to kill them off we dream a disease
mixo gives them milk for eyes gauze over the retina over the landscape
you can't see straight blind ahead
a feral people—introduced
deb ball I didn't participate in the dance but I knew all the steps
the lace, the gauze, the muslin of the dress
white homestead fantasy—scarlet on the stairs
bride of big boss man in the big country
went out west (bless)—left the amenity

a colony in the body —how does it feel?

The Grasscutters

Jo Gardiner

The crescent moon—a silver
fish turning out of night's current—
trawls the sheaves
of shadow—that part of you

*

always waiting for the end
when you will have used
up all the slow grace given—
the tulip tree

*

where you sit while Jess, Nuni
and Axel make coffee,
its bones fine
as a gazelle's hollow,

*

unbranched horns—
and you try to shrug yourself
free of forceps, scalpel,
and the bone drill—your debt

*

of sorrow—playing in your head
like the demented tune
of the coal train
shrieking down the line,

*

fear sitting like jellied
marrow in your bones
but, again, your body
becomes plangent, poignant

*

inside thin skin gone brown—
a pear left too long
in the basket.
Units of measurement

*

that make a difference
you're told, may be
as miniscule as a key fob,
a ferrule or plastic wedge

*

slipped under the body's steep
slope. Then, after the grass-
cutters shred long stems of light
along the road

*

to the pool, reaping
from morning's pasture
deep armfuls of gold leaf,
the swim—unanchored

*

from the pain of weight borne,
below wind and high cirrus
and two cumulus clouds
reaching toward each other,

*

arms outstretched in a Sistine Chapel
gesture. And you recall
the grasscutters,
and light—that placid

*

mentor to the heart—
waves slender fingers
through water
with nothing of the economy

*

of stillness you've been
practising so long now
since you fell
into this body hungry for motion

*

as the nomadic red wattlebird
with its brush-tipped tongue
is for the honey
blossoming in banksia and gum

*

like benevolence—the word
unfolds its tender hands over
limbs rubbed with sweet
touch and scented oil

*

wrung from leaves
drowsed into a fugue
state by bees—and with open
palms you turn in the water

*

with all your bones
singing, and arrive somewhere,
the moon faint
over your shoulder

*

and fading at the edge,
and the sun, coming on
strong, takes the song
on from here—

Lake Days

Andrew Menken

1. *LIV LIFE ALIVE*

A fish plips out, then plops
back into the water
like a luminous silver Pluto
Pup; the capillary waves
of its brief breach
in the breezeless dusk
mirror how both children
and astronomers sketch
the orbits of planets.

Somebody is taking a piano
lesson in the lakeside house
whose footings fall away
among the entangled
strings of lantana that choke
the embankment. Last week
a neighbour stopped

to warn me about a baby
brown snake he spotted
slinking out of and slithering
back into the tall grass;
I cut my stroll short that night
and almost shed my skin
when the bushes rustled.

This week I used a stick
to flick a very dead rat
off the bicycle track;
a woman scurried past
and nodded a thank you
like I was an ostiary
who got the door on cue.

Beyond the galahs
and our resident Willie
Wagtails, the Bigwigs
swirl, then swill red wine
in their swanky abode,
which is half glass
and was clearly half built
with Bauhaus in mind.

I'm soon confronted
again by the man whose air-
brushed and blown-up head
surfaces every few streets
on a piece of plastic
that has *FOR SALE*
or *SOLD* or *JUST SOLD*
slapped across its middle;
the stream of elegant homes
spits me out at the jetty,
where a fisherman dribbles
as he drowses and drifts

in his dory. It's too cool now
for the teens who lope
along the bridge and leap
from its rail to shatter
their shadow selves;
the horns of passing
trucks and goading shouts
of their occupants
no longer whirl above
the cold ear of the lake.

Nothing really changes
or moves in this space
between the thicket of oil-

stained pizza boxes
and the concrete pier
that bears what must be
a graffitied parody
of the cheesy mantra
LIVE LAUGH LOVE.

I'm starting to see things
for what they are
when the sunset scatters
the blue light once more
and the unwavering
song of a black field cricket
ripples through the park.

2. The Flies Have Gotten into the Dog Food

Emily Dickinson: I heard a Fly buzz

The flies have gotten into the dog food.
They cluster like atoms at the bottom
of the bag. This puncture appeared when Sam,
whose breezy life would madden Hesiod,

raised his caviar-coloured head and found
no hand to feed him one stormy autumn
afternoon. Each lightning flash took the form
of a biblical umbilical cord,

fusing Heaven with the waters that hide
God's slimy creations. I drop my dumb
duct-tape stratagem once the bag becomes
a Hadean crèche where a maggot horde

learns its limbless crawl. Like the rarefied
tide from Friedrich's vision of the sublime,
a morning mist floods the Mountain of Chum
I dump in the bin and drag to the road.

3. Some Sunday Mornings

an old man sells ferns on that stretch
of gravel where people park cars
for sale and bus drivers stop to nap
or smoke or eat lunch. The old man

scratches his shiny pate and smiles
in a way that says, 'I'm very *even-*
tempered and kind and *you're right*
it *is* rather cool for late October.'

Green beauties at five bucks each.
Every home looks better with a fern.
Find a spot with lots of filtered light.
Don't water her as much in winter.

Some Sunday afternoons an old man
folds his paper, rises from his chair
and ferries boxes of wispy plants
across churned-up stones to his van.

4. Town-Ships

Ishmael: Yes, as every one knows, meditation and water are wedded forever

Evacuation orders cold start the brains
of residents in Richards, Londonderry,
Ebenezer and the Lower Hawkesbury.

The Hawkesbury Gazette claims the rain
is easing and its fifteen-metre-high river
is falling. Notwithstanding, garden pots

and car lots have been *sub*plots since the knots
of thick clouds above Sackville, Windsor
and Richmond went slack. The SES,

who only just scoured the burning bushes
for signs of wildlife and scrubbed
the charred fur off their liveries,

shoulder shivering kids as God appears
busy recreating Genesis in medias res.
With Channel 7's logo in tow, a raft splits

the otoscope-like streetlights
to scoop up a woman who climbed
and clung to the closest tree (indefinitely)

after Noah was a no-show at Holsworthy.
Add Yarramundi, South Maroota West
and Agnes Banks to the swelling list

of Australian townships that are proving
to be more town than ship. A photograph
on *The Sydney Morning Herald* website

captures a border collie—stick in mouth—
prancing away from a Boston terrier,
whose pint-sized black-and-white head

drifts among florets of cauliflower
foam at Bronte Beach; what next?! A tern
fooling around with his gullfriend in a hot tub

of pointy rocks? Or perhaps some overfed
orange tabby surfing the barrel of a tsunami?
Business owners still afloat at Wollombi

jettison goods into box trailers and stack
sandbags against doors before they set sail
for drier ground; oh Lord! The Tavern,

which locals rechristened the Yacht Club,
is already sodden as a cabin boy's sock
and serving only patrons in tails and scales!

Warnings for Georges River, Woronora,
Pitt Town, Riverstone and parts of Portland
stream across my TV screen. When the bulk

carrier *Portland Bay* reels in the tempest
like a pickled hippo, her battery goes flat
and a thousand tonnes of coal-hued fluid

career towards the chip-toothed coast
at Royal National Park; a lone tugboat
with a skeleton crew lassoes the hulk

—a ghost crab hooking a colossal squid—
until two other tugs help drag the *Bay*
back out to sea. I nurse an Earl Grey

by a porthole in the rumpus room and watch
the RFS roll down our hill to ring the bells
of lakeside homes whose once top-notch

lawns are now low-end infinity pools;
under sheep-tinted skies and between drawn
blinds, they gleam like giant cobs of corn.

Families in Blue Haven, Chittaway, Long
Jetty, Tacoma, Rocky Point, Tuggerawong
(a hamlet its hermits call *God's Country*)

and the paludal palaces of Halekulani
scuttle through hallways-cum-canals,
hugging luggage and pieces of damp-

free furniture. In our normally quiet street
strangers cruise past slower than blimps
or reroute their constitutionals to meet

the Menace that lurks behind Nature;
stickybeaks flit about on a bitumen floe
while Gazza inspects the gunwales

of his leaky porch. Though we cast off
single-use plastics and clutch at paper
straws, the boffins tell us the future

will be a hellish half flash, half flood. Ergo,
unless the helm is frozen stiff or your skiff
is crude as a cannibal's coffin, you must steer

well clear of Lismore: the not-so-mythic
sunken city of the South Pacific.

5. Council Pick-Up

Oldies come and go
through her crap like she was Queen
of the Curio.

A Godwit Sonnet Cycle

Mark Tredinnick

1.

AT BURRILL LAKE, where first we saw the birds
   Who fly a feat each year, your life, my love,

Has made a daily practice of, the moon
   Is rosé pink and circus round, the tides

      Ride full and deep, but nowhere that we look
   At first are godwits where we hoped they'd be.

And on the second day I pick a calla
   Lilly from the bank behind the beach

      Around the point—your favourite flower. A sign,
   But not the kind the birds would be. And walking

Back, beside the dog, I watch the sky
   Cloud the way the estuary fills,

      And the breaking sea carries the night across
   The flats in one unbroken denouement.

2.

SOMEWHAT like the way a shepherd casts
  Her care across her flock, we scan the flats—

    Between the episodes of rain and work
  And barking dogs and all the care you take

Of me—for godwits. I think you think my mind
  Is everywhere but here with us; in truth,

    I'm working hard *not* to look for what
  We're hoping for so hard. The terns, ignoring

Health care etiquettes, crowd the sandbars
  As close as oysters on the rock the oyster-

    Catchers tend, and periodically
  They rise in a unison loose as a Mexican wave.

So like our hearts and markets, stalked by fear
  And flocked as quickly by ease. We watch the eagle

3.

ROUND the point and see the gulls and plovers
Fall to rest, the wagtails augur up

The night. And daybreak on day four is like
The batting of the burlesque lashes of

A god. And later on, the flats go farther
Under than I've ever seen them sink.

I float again upon the flood the thought
That good love will not come when called, but finds

You when it will, as love found us. So when
The waters fall, we run the dogs across

The corrugated sands, and is it any
Shock to anyone that *then* we see

Four godwits feeding where for days they'd been,
And all we ever had to do was give up

4.

HOPE—or set aside the need that crowds it
  Out. And love is being found by what

    You work to know you need, and Self appears
  To be more like a ragged constellation

Than a star, or so this tiny fellow-
  Ship of vagrants preaches to the dusk.

    Grace is unearned merit, but give it half
  A chance to show. And we've earned none

Of this, these stolen shores, whose middens speak
  Of all the wealth there was, and all the love

    That's lost. So, thank you, love, for letting ours
  Be found, for minding not too much how late

I ran: our anniversary's your birthday
  Now, and here's the estuary again.

Aeolian child

Jennifer Kornberger

1.

In the birth hour

your mother floats on an amniotic sea
your father's arms circle her like a life buoy

I sit to one side
entrusted with the birth plan

while you grind your way
through a tunnel, pausing
to read the inscriptions
on the wall

the obstetricians enter the labour room
bantering about team sports
marking out a football field
in this place of wombs

until your marble crown bourgeons
into a moon-white head

swiveling slowly on an unborn
column of flesh

the eyes not of an infant
turn to me in a movement
smooth as vernix

confirming the presence
and position of the actors
in this first cameo

before you breathe,
before the shock of air
takes you under

and delivers you
into your babyhood

before your life begins
as a babble of shadows

you permit me to see
the person who will
become the child

and then, as they pull
your body free

the cry comes
the little lament

because now you are a boy
to be measured and weighed
made one of the team

and I, clutching my authority
rise fierce into my first role

to stay the gowned men
for two pulsing minutes
before they cut the cord.

2.
Though your speech is late
you absorb intonation and inflection
as nutrients to store
in your slight musculature

your first sentence
a flock of waterbirds rising as one wing

I take this as a sign that you will resist
being given in fragments to the future;

and still, our anxiety waxes—
we see that you are cowed by noise
'hyperacusis' is the first title you accrue

you counter cacophony with your own soundscapes—
shrill dinning, long sequences of plosives

your speech wars with itself
consonants are shrapnel
diphthongs a sliding scale of anguish

you shift register to speak
in the guttural diablos
of invisible machines

'stimming' is the medico's name
for your vocal craft

a word too simple
too close to humming

no journal can explain
how you become aeolian
for baleful winds

I take this to mean
that you, like any poet,
must give voice to the stramash
that only you can hear;

who then, should silence

your desolate caterwaul?

You've seen through every clever
device to distract you

from giving us the intonation, the inflection
of a world in descending mode

as if you know the exact pitch of the vast
machinery, the virtual voices
that press to parent your future.

3.

You are assigned your place on the spectrum
somewhere between Defiance Disorder
and Demand Avoidance

a thin child who sprints
from the classroom door
you cannot be bribed with emoticons

you spy on dragonflies repairing
the tiny holes between
the warp and weft of air

notice when the cormorant
breaks the surface
how the river exalts
in the bone of its beak

observe too, how text messages are preceded
by the sound of distant rockfall

while other children complete
worksheets with known answers

you refuse to be photographed

to line up and wait
you refuse to leave your room;

the sky is full of silent thunder
the horizon a circle of cicadas

you live in the centre
of a persistent tinnitus

your screaming is followed
by the shock of true silence

in which you compass
the world's corpse.

4.

You demand to be taken to the river-mouth
so you can paddle out
and anchor your kayak
beyond our reach

from the shore we watch
you lower the chain

and when the metal umbilicus lodges
in the placenta of the riverbed

we entrust you to the only teacher you will accept—
we give you over to the wind

even now, we expect much
from your education

we hope, in the strict breeze pitching from the south
that you are learning the necessary phonics

the sequence of sounds
the order of words to speak

should the Earth become
a dead fruit hanging in space

we trust that you, savant of our survival,
will know how to reverse ruinous tides

and if the world is to be buried
we wish you able to intone
the lay that will bury it as a seed.

You remain motionless in the kayak
when we call you back to shore

sitting on your throne of water
just far enough beyond our demands
to make us uneasy

the wind low-voiced now
instructing you in how
to become unbiddable.

5.
Child, I do not know
how to end this poem

you've seen through every attempt
to resolve you into language

you have taught me to refrain
from pasting endings
that belong to previous drafts

I will remain keeper

of the birth plan

guard the cord that connects me
to your beginning

hold the question that the closed door
of your room persists in asking:
by what authority do you force me to do your will?

I am to watch for the slow arrival
of the person
before the first breath

the *you* who may muster
your long disobedience

to seize a living descant
from the Earth's death rattle

I can only accompany you
ready to intercede on your behalf

ask that you be forgiven
such stoic defiance.

The appeal of paint: A man waits for his execution

Sarah Rice

(After Myuran Sukumaran's exhibition *Another Day in Paradise*)

A peel
of paint
curls its lip
Coils itself small

Has already tied
itself in knots

Paint can wait it out
take its time
Drying is a lengthy business
dying far too quick

The paint is thick
like a leg or neck
It has an edge
and waits by it

In the final throws
how many of those paintings
had yet to dry
Still live

before the slow sealing over
of skin that grows on milk
The end
of silky stickiness

Fluidity remained
Things could still have been changed

The paint reworked
Nothing had set quite yet

The paint you see still flesh
fresh to the touch
could still be pressed
with finger or brush

An imprint left
A mark of some sort
Some thing could still be written
in its blood

A line could yet be drawn

Before each of them
slowly froze

Mama I built you up
stroke by stroke
as you did me
in you

cell by cell
A touch of baby blue
A note of pure orange
A pink pore

And for both of us caught
in this act of creation
This careful execution
The whites of our eyes showing

Mother I paint your eyes open
like an open mouth
Mama you held me small

Now hold the largeness of me

The unbearable largeness of me
My round power

I have green around my mouth
but my forehead is blessed with pinks
I wipe my mouth with this dirty flag
It smears my lips kissed with sweat

It catches in my throat
The flag flies in my mouth
in my fingers
in my face

I ask that my paintings
walk out with me
into the sunshine
Into the waiting space

My executioners cannot face
the myriad faces of me

Finials

Jennifer Harrison

I

In the bracket corners
of the cast iron fence
webs flourish and thicken   penny spiders
sewing space together

until the letterbox's slit mouth
has been absorbed by driftwood skeins
ragged with desiccated prey—
later you arrange six ruby Protea

in a huge optimistic vase
and notice the tendrilled slime
a week later climbing from the slush
of unfreshened water

II

The refrain from Goethe's poem 'Heidenröslein'
Röselein Röselein Röselein rot
Röselein auf der Heiden
is like a thorn echoing   nagging at a sleeve …

in a rethought work he allowed the boy
to leave the rose unplucked
its romantic meadow that way more exquisite
forever alive in memory's enchantment …

today you roam the neighbourhood
foraging for curbside wildflowers   while on the bookshelf
the blue cover of *German Verse* bleaches slowly
to a fluvial leaden grey

III

German Verse (1969) by Schultz and Samuel—
the rasp-harshness of language—
a flint grinding at the edge of stone—but you remember
how Heinrich Heine's Belsazar

recoiled from those prescient words
written in black smoke on the palace wall—
an omen that only Daniel could read
before the glyph faded

leaving the banquet guests
afraid that what they had once seen there
might never be forgotten   jewelled goblets raised
midline   midlife   midway

IV

Protea don't wither like lavender
or wilt like tulips
they peer alive from death   spines stiffening
arthritically

into parchment skirts
so thistle-sharp and grimly petalled
their tawny dry shadow-sticks
seem thick with the memory of ships

voyaging across green glassy seas …
South African imports
they thrive among the pamphlet maps
rooms-to-let   roof tiling jobs

V

Buy-swap-and-sell
advertisements for recycled slate and bluestone

Speedy Jim electrical repairs … seem less meaningful
than a spider's tiny trypanosomic fangs

feasting on garden biology—
life's flutter   trapped and shrivelling—
in Hölderlin's 'Hyperions Schicksalslied'
sun and earth were spun

from the one apocalyptic theology
an answer to *der Knabe's* self-lyric
benignly bright   throbbing nostalgically
on the reiterative spring branch—

Hölderlin's poem
bore indentations like *Klippe* stepping down the page
in sharp-edged diminishment
a winged Satan   carved into words

split by a master mason
the chisel placed precisely along the fault line
of a verse   a protea   a finial—
carcass or a husk   I wonder

VI

You think you've given all
to language like a trapped insect
as you lie across an unmade bed
the pearl buttons of your dress

glinting   the house bobbing
along the tide of time's rank water
(the way rain leaks into the kitchen through the skylight
when a storm comes from the west)—

today the windows are dry
and as motionless as dead eyes

the house becoming ever more brittle
        from the inside out   but everlasting—

                Kim and I attended
        Adult Education German classes
the limo picking us up from school each Thursday
        her moody sadness a kind of flower too—

                yesterday I googled her
        but couldn't find a single rose   no trace   no web
she'd vanished like the leaves of the ornamental pears
        their branches more naked each winter

At sixes and sevens

Greg McLaren

1. As if

It's not as if it happened to me.
The sly nod and a drink, a joint. Then the hands.
Those heavy, valley-wide clouds, pressing down.
Where are the lines, between one thing and another?

The nod and a sly drink, a joint, his hands down your pants.
Little wonder I'm hyper-vigilant.
What lines are there, between the one thing, another?
The silos and rail bridges on Sunday drives.

You might wonder why I'm so vigilant.
Panicked plovers in the stormless night,
silos alongside rail bridges, Sunday drives.
Scout ranks in the War Memorial's shade.

What panicked the storm birds last night?
The light this time of day, rain on the grass,
the Scouts in the War Memorial's shade,
the back-and-forth glancing to the car park.

The light, this time of day. Light on the grass.
Events keep returning, despite precautions.
Back-and-forth pacing, eyes on the car park,
looking for a safe path away from here.

Events keep returning, despite the medication.
The future, invisible, a throbbing migraine.
Looking for anywhere safe, anyone, any time,
but there are blanks where memory should be.

The future, invisible. A migraine pulses in,
clouds pressing down, across the valley,
masking blanks where memory should be.
It's not as if, as she said, it happened to me.

2. Don't touch

And how I survived those boys, I don't know.
When the oleander avenue blossomed: *Don't touch.*
Join the circus, the army, turn carny and go.
She invited him into the house, oblivious.

Don't touch! when the oleanders were in bloom.
Thumping of the waves. Artillery. Getting hit.
She invited him into the house, oblivious.
Try to make yourself seem bigger. Carry a knife.

Thumping of the waves. Artillery. Learn to get hit.
She picked up sympathetic magic, let down their tyres—
make yourself seem bigger, conceal your knife.
Golden hour pours through the trees out the back.

He learnt sympathetic magic, spiked their tyres.
It's not winter yet. The engine won't turn over.
Golden hour pours light through the trees outside of town.
As if stealing's no way to make a living.

Not yet even winter, the fucken car won't turn over.
Mindful: how revenge fantasies mutate and spin,
as if thieving's no way to keep staying alive.
It's not easy to say one way or another.

I don't mind how my revenge fantasies mutate and spin.
Join the circus, the army, turn carny and go.
It's not easy to say one way or another.
How I survived those boys? I still don't know.

3. Small nips from the plums

Each night takes small nips from the plums.
Sandstone and shales—time piled on time.
Potholes collapse at the edges, dated notions of sovereignty.
Next door's flag slack and bright as an emptied goon.

Sandstone and shales—time keeps piling on time.
Luxurious normality, though smoke's wafting everywhere.
Their flag slack and bright as an emptied goon.
The frogmouth's wingtip brushed the windshield.

Farewell, luxurious normality—smoke wafting everywhere.
Raking up leaves, the helicopter trailing its bladder.
The frogmouth's wingtip brushed the windshield.
A leaf-blower pushing the sand back off the road.

Raking up leaves, and a single helicopter trailing its bladder.
Bees in the sage, my ringing ears, the world's echolalia.
A leaf-blower pushing sand back off the beach road.
The bush shaking its canopy like a rattle.

Bees in the sage late, my ears ringing at the world's echolalia.
Distant rivers gurgle dry into cracked longwalls,
the bush shakes its brown canopy like a tambourine.
Around the corner, traffic's loud aspirin, getting out.

Distant rivers gurgle dry into cracked longwalls.
Calyptorhynchus at the nursing home.
Around the corner, traffic's loud aspirin, getting out.
Corellas dismantle the main drag's gums.

Calyptorhynchus funereus at the nursing home.
Potholes collapse at the edges, like dated notions of sovereignty.

Corellas dismantle the main drag's gums.
Each night takes small nips from the plums.

4. Spill and eddy

All this constant moving through the dark,
the unlit river snapped in strobes, in distant lashes of light.
Any map of this would be a wavering blur.
Constellations spiral and wheel, hazard lights flicker between the trees.

The unlit river snapped in strobes and flashes of distant light.
Make sure your fire is out before you leave.
Constellations spiral and wheel. Hazard lights between trees.
Mist comes rolling through, or maybe smoke: give it time.

Make sure your fire is out before you leave, and
head for the mountains, watch who moves in the valleys.
Mist comes rolling through, or maybe smoke: just give it time.
Tent-splayed sportsgrounds in each town, all flapping edges.

Head for the mountains, watch who moves in the valleys.
These times, I guess, might spill and eddy back onto someone other's.
Tent-splayed sportsgrounds in each town flap at the edges,
but don't pity me—look up instead as the ironbarks bloom.

Any time, I guess, could spill and eddy back into another.
Sitting out here with the dog, the sun feels a little like love.
Don't pity me—look up instead at the ironbarks as they bloom.
The last night up there, looking out over the plain, its bright sweep of dust.

Sitting out here with the dog, the sun feels a little like love
after all this constant moving through the dark.
The last night up there, looking out over the plain, its bright sweep of dust,
Though any map you try using folds out into a wavering blur.

5. Black Swan Motel

Dogs' nails on the back deck. Heels approaching.
Cockatoos drop and flap their sandy towels.
Clear sky, but currawongs cheer on the rain,
the piano next door grinding its teeth.

Cockatoos drop and flap their sandy towels.
I sit writing pantoums, reviving trauma.
The piano next door is grinding its teeth.
Jean's photo of black swans on the lake at twilight

as I sit writing pantoums, repeating trauma, relieving
it, making patterns that spiral then fade a while.
A polaroid of black swans on the twilit lake,
reading *Batman* all week at the Black Swan Motel:

pattern the hurt, let it spiral then fade for a while,
and return. So many things were yet to have happened.
That week at the Black Swan Motel by the swamp,
the shoreline reeds, the muck that covers what it covers.

So many things I wish had not happened.
Now, the dogs yap and yap into our birdless backyard, but still
those reeds screen the shoreline, the muck covering up whatever,
because someone refused to stay in that fucking van again.

The dogs yap and yap at our birdless backyard.
The wireless, she said, turn down the bloody wireless.
Someone refused to stay one more fucking night in that van,
its hot vinyl smell, the cockroaches ticking all night.

The wireless, she said, turn the wireless bloody well down.
The sky's clear for now, but currawongs cheer on the coming rain.
No hot vinyl smell, only the clock's hushed ticking at night.

Dogs' nails on the back deck. The hills look as if approaching.

6. Flawed codices

If there was a time machine and invisible ink I'd drive
along these back hills roads smudged with what might be fox,
these long meandering lines knotted with quips and in code.
On the podcast, something about living in a haunted house,

in the shade of black hills, the roads there smudged with fox,
the poor benighted locals driving home late from the TAB,
and on the podcast, something about living in a haunted house.
I've been putting on the sorrow, drinking in new bars.

The poor bin-nighted locals driving home late from the shops,
crossing the range, its back roads, on one headlamp
while I've been putting on sorrow, drinking in bars.
Here I go, whispering out my heart's flawed codices,

crossing the range and its back roads on the one headlamp.
My preference is always self-sabotage—don't you see?
Here, have another go at my art-flawed codpiece,
gaze at these yellow-rimmed windows from the rear lanes.

My preference is always self-sabotage—didn't you see me,
muttering out failure on the steps to your door, eyes
half-glazed, looking at these yellow-rimmed windows.
If I had anything still left to tell you, I would,

not muttering my failure on the steps to your door, eyeing
off these long meandering lines knotted with quips, part in code.
If I had anything still left to tell you, I would.
If I had a time machine and invisible ink, I would.

7. Discarded boys

A time machine and a bundle of twine,
a copy of his house keys, a tin of kerosene,
a baseball bat wound with barbed wire, and a mask.
Approaching rain flicks on its chuckling birds.

Copy his house keys, pour a tin of dad's kerosene.
Hide the burn marks on your skin: all those matches.
Approaching rain screens out its clutter of birds.
Climb the hill, keep an eye on anything moving below.

Hide the burn marks on your skin. All those matches,
the hurt that liberates, that lifts you out of one moment, almost.
Climbing the hill, keep an eye on anyone moving.
We grew up saying *th* as an *f*, from class solidarity, or somefing.

Hurt can nearly liberate, lifting you out of that moment.
Go outside, sit in the sun. Stay there, tracking the shade.
We grew up saying *th* as an *f*, from class solidarity, or somefing.
Under the backyard back there, the buried pets, their grave goods.

Go outside, sit in the sun. Stay there, tracking the shade.
The anti-bullying program boiled down to *Don't be such a poof.*
Under the backyard there, the secretly buried pets, their stash of grave goods,
The double-stuttered lined-up remembering, brain's tourniquet.

The anti-bullying program? *You're a little poof. Start running.*
Discarded boys left behind at the library, the zoo, with the pederast.
This double-shuttered memories, my brain turns a key.
The boxy church's uplights, hue of unflickering flame.

Left behind at the library, the zoo, at home with the pederast:
get my own back with a time machine and a bundle of twine,
His boxy church's uplights, a hue of unflickering flame.
My kingdom for a length of barbed wire, for a tin of kerosene.

Plissken in the City

Elena Gomez

I'm enjoying lately the buoyancy
  of desire
The briefcase shackled to my wrist
contains certain secrets

My state anoints me where was
once a requirement of self-destruction is now

Strong, urgent need
                  to be destroyed by another

   or by the wants of another

This is a poem about presidents

but I am a president I am about it: the
imprisonment, unpaid labour
imperial resource extraction and the point
when the tight black stretch tank top
wraps around Snake Plissken's quite large shoulder

I had the briefcase I was
all for this plan see

Snake's long locks are around somewhere too

Yes I am the president, the vice chancellor
 I am the warehouse owner
I'm also thinking about Snake Plissken's
  icy blue iris

but it's this: a tendency
towards the rate of desire

of labour reserve army management &
carceral state cosplaying as care

  it was no escape but rescue
mission

We love nuclear fusion
in this house
 but I also love
to keep
occupied in ways

such as observing
the filled & fitted grey
camo tights
worn by our Snake

such as listening to the huge heart
in my chest that beats for him

your hero has arrived in the city
your hero will unspool a cassette

I am the president but I am also lovely

It's step aside in time
for they call themselves
The 69th international

Before then our black
tank tops were factorymade

distributed on long trucks
& sung about by orville peck

You were asked this: what is a president?

I have a large ring

Also they call it a thick wrist, good for a shackle

My briefcase against global peril

This was a poem for Snake Plissken's tank top

We tried the recreation, large nail-stud
bats

What we call the working day
for unpaid labour or like, escape from
surplus labour extracts

~

I came here to work on my crushes
  But the synths are very loud and present

How they say

      a Mood

My object is Snake
 Flexed traps

The problem with being the president is this
The revolution

The problem is that the poem as a form
is coming to an end for all time

Let's say how it does end

We were rescued from a vat
We scooped ingredients for our
attack poem, a sort of cross

Between a jus and a sauce or
Sort of like a thick chutney
 If you ask me

We filled the commons pulled
Out tapes
  Unspooled time

At a crucial but inevitable moment the appearance of Harry Dean Stanton

This is also the point I reveal that there in one corner you find
Where it is Springsteen who is on fire where Brooks has laid it out
  Steeped us, prepared the space
While over here in another corner is
the same room but it's this:
Blood and dirt and dirt and dirt and blood

                    And blood

I'm not pretending I'm
  in love with Snake for selfish
reasons but of course
it would be nice to have
my ringed finger returned

Not for the finger but
 For the stone
inside the ring

The Keeper of the Field

Mal McKimmie

I am the knower of the field in everyone, Arjuna.
Knowledge of the field and its knower is true knowledge.

The Bhagavad Gita
Trans. Eknath Easwaran, Nilgiri Press, 1985.

I am a keeper of sheep.
The sheep are my thoughts
And my thoughts are all sensations.

The Complete Works of Alberto Caeiro, Fernando Pessoa,
Ed. Jeronimo Pizarro & Patricio Ferrari,
Trans. Margaret Jull Costa & Patricio Ferrari,
New Directions, 2020.

I have no ambition or desires.
Being a poet is not my ambition.
It's my way of being alone.

The Complete Works of Alberto Caeiro

Like Alberto Caeiro, who existed
without existing and did so splendidly,
stewarding the ruminants grazing
the green mind of Fernando Pessoa,
I never kept sheep, but it's as if I did.
As if I unstintingly cared for and
watched over the woolly projections of
a poet's mind and, like all such shepherds,
thought these chimeras real and my charges.
What happened, I do not really know,
but after a long and troubled sleep
(perhaps like my old friend Gregor Samsa's),
I woke to a field as verdant as ever
but empty of thoughts, empty of sheep.

~

Why does the silence of an empty field
frighten the poet? Do I really wish
a part in the concrete, cacophonous,
congratulatory world? Is the ripe field
of simple awareness, the mind *sans* thoughts,
worth so little? Is simple awareness
simple? … I am an old insomniac
who got himself to sleep by counting sheep
as they leapt, one by one, over the fence
(if there's a field, there's definitely a fence).
Is it my fault that my thoughts about my thoughts
turned out to be, in their fashion, true?
I was less shepherd than witness anyway.
And now I am the keeper of the field.

How to *keep* this sheepless, empty field
may be beyond me. But if I have dreamt it
(and I have), then so it must be. God help me.
God help me list what I must not forget:
The sheep never belonged to the poet,
that was illusion; the field gives rise to
the sheep: in breeding and birthing, grazing
and growing, the field is the true shepherd;
the grass and even the cantankerous
weeds in the field, the roots of grass and weeds,
the water those roots find underground,
the water that falls from the sky's blue field,
the light from sun and moon and stars—these are
the true keepers of sheep. And these are fields.

~

Keeping this field seems both more difficult
and more effortless than anything I
have ever done. At times it also seems
unnecessary. If effortlessness is the key,
where is the keeping and why a keeper?
Why any keeper? Why not just the field?
And why, O why, the sheep in the first place?
And this poet who bred, bought or invented
them; or just found them bumping amiably
around in his head? … Because there are too
many questions to ask, it's best not to
ask any questions at all—if the weight
is too much, keeper, get down on your knees
in the grass with a pair of nail scissors!

Today, in a corner of the field,
I found the four bones of the poet—
I, me, my, and mine—in a cruciform
arrangement. I had to laugh! Even in death,
I bang on about my sacrifice.
There is no resurrection, and there is
definitely no ascension. Without sheep,
the field is what and where it needs to be.

And I tend it well, this field; the death
of the poet being necessary for
poetry, and the emptiness of the field
the beginning of tomorrow's fullness.
I realise now just how sick and tired
I was of all those flocks of bleating sheep!

~

These lyrics appear on the empty field
munching noiselessly, paradoxically.
I do not know what animal they are,
but I do know what animal they're not.
They come and go like the rain and the wind,
grazing only briefly, if at all, as if
they do not need the field (or its keeper).
If silence were a genus, these lyrics
would be a species belonging to it.
I used to spin like a top just to stay
upright; now I lie on my back, listening
to grass grow. Sometimes these lyrics wander
as clouds across the sky, then disappear.
They are transient, like love or happiness.

Did I say this field has a fence? Well, it
doesn't anymore. It seems the fence came
down, was taken down, or disappeared
with the sheep, as if they were interdependent
(I faintly recall a lyric passing
through here, singing something along these lines).
Given the absence of a fence, where is
the distinction between this field and another?
Do I tend a disappearing border?

Leaves of grass, field to field, lean in sympathy,
mirror each other; flowers too; even
weeds copy their kin; creepers creep towards
each other; and roots, well, roots have always known:
nothing is alone, nothing under the sun.

~

Nothing is alone, not even me.
Everything is interdependent:
every seemingly single thing depends
on every other seemingly single thing;
like roots entwined, regardless of surface
appearance. How do poets *not* know this?
And that because of this interdependence,
every individual object,
every single 'thing', is as empty
of an individual identity
as this field is now. This includes the poet,
who is an object, a thing, and whose
mind is a field (sheep or silence) with its
origin the body—which is a field.

The field is green, the earth is made of fields,
the earth is green (the sad poet was not),
I suspect the heart of the universe is green …
I shall tend this silence for a long time;
be its servant, its keeper. If lyrics
pass me by, like clouds in the lost and found
of the sky, what's a book less in the world
but silence? And which is needed more?

Awareness demands all my awareness:
sometimes I wish I didn't have to sleep.
Duty should be enough to sustain me.
But the question nags: Have I ceased to be
one thing without becoming another?
The Knower of the Field does not answer.

~

I do not know the Knower of the field,
but I suspect the Knower knows me well.
I have just begun to keep the field (now
that it is free to keep, and I am free,
so to speak, to keep it) … I get a glimpse,
every now and then, of what it's like
when everything's one field and one field
only that extends to the horizon.
There, storm clouds gather (it needs watering);
between these clouds a light opens like a
narrow door. An upheaval in my life
seems on its way, seems unavoidable.
'I wish I did' and 'I wish I didn't'
fall away—I wish I'd got here sooner.

If I had got here sooner, then perhaps
knowing the Knower would seem possible.
Perhaps it never does (that narrow door).
I wish I kept the field in which religion grew.
Poetry might be my way of being
alone, but I know I'm not alone—I've
always known. Some poets have this problem.
As if knowledge of the shadows that words cast
daily shadows the poet until
fully embracing silence is the only option.
I am not sure if I wish this for you;
I once had a choice, but it's long gone.
I hear a happy brook murmuring, *Wait.*
But I will meet the Knower or will not.

Region / Ritual

Claire Albrecht

It was almost six months before I
heard about the hairy panic. I'd been
living darkly, closing my windows
to the canola and the wasps,
reading about errant cows and yowies
and learning the turns of my neighbours.

It's like a tumbleweed, the panic.
A grass that dries and takes off:
down highways, dirt roads, up past
doorsteps. Suffocating the chipboard cottage
right up to the doors, the windows,
or eating sheep up whole in the sunset.

It's witchgrass, a ritual,
a hand across your mouth.
Moth wings. Gecko feet on the window.

I spent our first Spring here hiding my legs
under thick black tights, jeans, long dresses.
Not ashamed, exactly, but certain that
in supermarkets, on the karaoke stage,
on the bowling green, in the front yard,
those sparse dark hairs would give me away.

And now each afternoon, under smoke-sky,
the hairy panic is a reminder,
like bowls rolling by, like a death mask,
a mirage, a miracle. That this Country
isn't lonely, ever. And, therefore,
I cannot be lonely.

Consider: the stubble quail
by the side of the road, pecking
at the hairy panic. Swallowing
the dryness down like a delicacy.

Consider: dense patches in the dry.
The ritual burning of canola crops
that match-stick up the landscape.

Consider: hairy panic, when consumed
by livestock, can photosensitise.

Consider: there are six smoke shops here
and no book shop.

Consider: no one cares
if you shave your legs.

Consider: you are very unlikely
to be buried alive.

Controlled Burn

A. Frances Johnson

1. Practice burn

The silent man, her neighbour,
who is always paid more for less,
stock and field, has a mouth full
of clattering silver, jowls that shudder
pilgrim entitlement, gouty wrath.
His stony silence is different to the
skeined smoke blanketing the valley.
He choreographs rollies in quiet,
practised strikes. With other men,
he's loquacious, a trough tap turned on.
He calls them all up—her practice burn
must be argued against, her stream access.
Fire is bitch, as he sees it, controlled burns
a fool's idea. By Christ, he repeats,
but he can't make it rhyme.
His neighbour is a bad spot fire,
something to be put out, like those
mucking up the river pasture
in his grandad's rifling time.

But he underestimates her cool
melancholy, how science and law
undergird her decision not to sell,
to stay and defend. She won't be put out.
Let him suck the fire brigade dry,
let the world burn uncontrolled.
There's no room in her bunker for him.

2. The woman who ran the farm

Anger and fire race faster uphill.
Introduce a slope of small
degree and wildfire burns
a quick path to the wooden desk.
Introduce a clever woman.
See her forecast inquisitions
of fiery words. She's raced
past two dead husbands—
each liked a bet and a pint,
a purpling Rorschach punch.
She knows the burnt parts
of history, spot fires of disbelief
connect her canopy of days
to the fencepost's grey desperation.
She races past her hot tin sheds;
their pinging siren songs won't save.
She can't outrun the livid forest,
a season of fuse and tripwire.
Still, she limits her sprint and
segments fate, trading chances.
Running towards the boiling lake,
she frees butting stock en route.
The creatures' sideways eyes
rim with panic and woolly trust.
Wire cutting slows her down,
hands blistering, shins
smouldering in yellow grass.

Mask askew, she recalls documents,
chaste and white, on the dash
of the exploding ute. Hear her
howl at this rare stupidity.
Call it temperament, call her victim,
crazy-for-not-leaving. Call her witch.
She won't leave her animals, won't sell
cheap to the jawless neighbour.
Now the cattle are lakeside,
alive and safe. Soon she'll be with them.
But the candled understorey
closes in, a birthday surprise.
The lake disappears, a distraught mouth.
In the north paddock, furies rise,
throats buttoned down by fire.
Her mother and grandmother
have each played their bitter part
and handed it to her, as if this was always
the place to start, run from and finish in.
Wear an ironed blouse, they wail,
compact earth is a devil's dancefloor.
This is it, she thinks, dam bubbling
vestigial hope, the calves' stricken choir
renouncing teats, grassy memory.
She sprints through ash and smoke,
a singed Diana, if only to be
her last, best potential, fuelled by
a sleep of dreams, young animals
lowing, calling her to green pastures.

boiled potato makes me gag

J Marahuyo

Part 1

I've taken a year round trip
back to the date of
my one of a kind abortion.

I was too nauseous to be nervous, or
rather, awfully nauseous, a little nervous and
looking forward to it.
The anaesthetist gave me
a task, count up to 10. I made it
to two. The anti-nausea
turned my poop
to moss for a week.

(

)

Back from the ether
I was greeted by a nurse
and an indecipherable question
which after several attempts
my brain finally registered as
'Would you like some tea?'

(
...
)

Here I am, precisely one year on with
a woman I've never met asking, 'So
when are you having a baby?'

'I have one already
Frankie, my cat', I reply.
She nibs at my younger sister
as she says 'My first at your age
jabs in my air
'My second at yours and my
third last year.

You need a baby.' Oh,
makulit Tita how I wish
I kept my tiny
vacuumed foetus as a talisman
wore it around my neck to
ward off people like you.

Part 2

(
;
)

To be honest, I've always coddled my dream:
my own children. So, I entertained
your beginning, asked if we should keep you
but his no turned into mine.

10 days after conception
I felt, what my mind could only describe
as a little black ping pong
snug in my uterus.

During my 8 weeks of pregnancy
I was not tired.
I was barely.
My body craved horizontality.

I could smell the posters on the wall.
Water had an aftertaste.

The only things I could eat were crackers
a banana
the cool air.

I woke several times in the night
from the foetus' feckless father's
rancid coffee induced
gastro-oesophageal reflux.

I thought pregnancy would be
the death of me.

(

.

)

He said when we're ready I better
find a way to be less weak
be less boiled potato makes me gag
be less overwhelmed by just being awake
be less all my clothes make me feel heavy, I can feel the
seams, they're scratching my skin
be less lose 3kg
be less please clean the stove I can smell it across the
apartment

He said it was a horrible experience
for him
he didn't want to go through such worry again.

I took an Uber to the clinic.

The Thought Eagle

Jennifer Kornberger

Every eagle poem you've got
is here, a double space
of sky between them

that is how far an eagle sees
from one page to the next

its new haunt the peak moment
before a line break

with no qualification other than
general anxiety, you offer
the wingspan of words

to write the bird onto the shoulder of this day
a day being two horizons
and the scarp that connects them

where you walk in the late sun
your shadow lurching ahead of you

when the eagle's shadow slides
alongside yours on the chalk path
before veering off, and you,

willing to be prey to its circadian vision
watch it angle towards you again, this time it glides
over your loping umbra—your head, at the last
moment, is briefly winged.

In this mating of shadows
you hope to acquire
an aerial perspective to quell
your rodent response to life—

even the fear of having your fear
snatched from you.

*

The local precipice
is the edge of your child's bed

where the fruit of your exhausted womb
refuses to sleep until you have
answered his vertiginous question,
what do you do when you die?

What infuriates him is the idea of rest
the inaction of the dead

unless you are confident
of a worthy, bodiless vocation,
he threatens chronic insurrection.

You know that your reply
will determine the final
shape of his heart, the depth
of his lungs, the fortitude of his blood.

The wild jury of the eagle is in his eye,
tonight, you will become his mother
or orphan him—force him
to search outside your prevarication

for ways to scale the scarp
soar into the panorama.

*

The reason for adopting the 'you' form
(you explain to your editor)
is the wish to distance yourself from the first person—

its claim to be sole
author of any instance

for too long the 'I' has capitalised
on its selfdom, closed itself off
from the influence of weather

reduced the world to a single stroke.

You describe how, at its wingtips,
the eagle becomes air
feathering into the hands of the wind

its cry is a high pitched 'you'
and again, 'you'
as it twists into the above

re-emerging as the first thought
of the mountain, courier between summits

it can only know itself
between call and response

only survive in the atmosphere
of the second person.

*

In one draft, you are eaten by the eagle,
you note a palpable sense of relief
sometimes located in dreams—

finally, you have secured an afterlife
before the fact, you have become part

of the eagle's slow circling
above the centrepoint of any day;

this, you suspect, is the secret
ambition of your fear.

*

The writing group is uneasy

T. says the gradient of the poem is too steep
suggests you include more horizontal material
drawn from lived experience.

You appease your colleagues
your senses bow five times

you allow your memory to bloom
like an orchid—half spider, half flower,

from its olfactory archive
the nose retrieves the smell of the sun
in the forest at North Walpole

a fume of scarlet resin, hint of formic
acid, one cloying note of nectar, astringent
leaf green, base of smoked granite

there you are on a desultory hunt
for the Queen of Sheba orchid
with a friend and her mincing dog

an eagle drifts over the cornea of the sky
becomes an eyelash, floating out of sight

when the cicadas pause in their roundelay
the eagle returns, carrying a grey
tree limb in its talons

circles the dog
drops the branch too late

the clatter-shuck of wood
on rock echoes from Mt. Franklin

the bird carefully wipes itself
from the corner of your eye.

In that country the eagle
has two names, certain duties

it's possible you were loitering
without true intent

trespassing on the integrity
of its patch of sky.

*

There is another eagle
the same one that bloodied
your ancestor Prometheus

after he woke the infant human race
from its torpor—

the thought eagle that must descend
to tear at your liver as soon as you wake
and begin to burn the fuse of your life

it is the price
for possessing fire
the bright roar of the mind
the conflagration called consciousness.

Only in sleep when thinking is doused
can the bird recoil from its curse

weep its dark dew over your liver
watch the organ bloom back

fold its ragged wings
over your nakedness

over the heart which is still
finding its final shape.

You clasp the eagle in sleep
and it drenches you in other vistas

suggests ways to outgrow this myth

things that memory will not
retain in daylight;

at dawn, it lifts its beak
heavy with reluctance

begins again its gory task.

This too, is your lived experience.

*

One day soon, the child you gave birth to
will walk along a precipice in the Metaverse

he will be offered a home there
another set of senses

every artificially intelligent day
will last thirty minutes.

Before this happens, you will travel
with him to Italy, on the last holiday
of his childhood

to the mountains at Tarvisio
which rise as huge, shorn heads—ears, eyes,
slow cascades of scree

mouths dribbling into one dry riverbed
white rocks a necropolis of teeth

you will wander, with your son,
amongst the headstones of Earth
climbing the shoulder of day

your talk high and spare
the eagle appearing to hang on your words.

What you said to him when he was four,
your answer to his question
is now climbing with you

as the invisible third person
whose vocation is to lead the explorer
hand over hand, out of the frozen waste

the companion at the sheer face
who shows you where to place your foot
in the fall of rocks

where to step next
in a crumbling world.

The Honey Room

Jo Gardiner

… the knowledge of impermanence that haunts our days
is their very fragrance—Rilke

ON BROKEN Rock Ridge in Woodford,
just below the snow line, the first wintry
morning at the end of another fall:
one more than you deserve; one more
than you thought you'd know. One more swivel
of the chisel through a canyon carved from a block
of blue air. Stand anchored to earth
in a place to fly
or fall from, or pitch off in another direction, high
enough now to see all the twists and turns. The moon's
a pale fish sliding through a net of stars flung across

the night; waves of breath beside you break
open summer's harvest groomed by the Nubian bee—
memory read frame by frame,
each flowering the acres
of time—when light struck the violet-petalled eye
of a bowerbird watching you from inside a tibouchina,
when you woke to paddocks silvered with frost,
or sat with a book in a walnut tree and broke open
the shell of language
to find inside the secret life of honey
its amber smell. In the room right at the bottom
of this old house, a lime-green breeze through

an open window lifts dust from your feet—the touch
of places, traces of pollen brought back
to home base. Dip a spoon into swirls of nectar,

steal back time
even as night waits under
the pines to croon its songs of disquiet
into the body's dusk. Some days play a music
we can't sing to, so we must sit
in the lost temple space of the heart,
and like bees overwintering,
warm our hands at the hearth
of other people's lives and feed on kindness—

the animal comfort of company. Before the smoulder
of their fire, like singers of the epics with each stanza
written on a pebble
in a pile in the mind, we break into our hoard
of memory and draw a comb from the store.
Each of the seasons we've lived—as some other version
of ourselves—is hived within us,
each leaf or bud sealed in beeswax
and kept from the alchemy of ordinary time.
Above the folded rim of the blue canyon,
along the highway heading north of Katoomba,
the old oaks kneel before you, the sun

snags in waves of giant poplars banking gold, and every
breath breathed edges you closer to the furnace
when each grief will be the last. Through morning
haze, follow the turning of the crescent
moon, the learning curve of the sky's wing
reaching out to the world.
Step past the hive guards into the room outside
the door: a Blackheath street where, arms raised to trees
and light, a man at the crossing circles in private
adulation, his jacket yellow as a beech leaf.
If a blessing walks toward you, stop and meet it.

Night Music Under the Sign of the Platypus

Shari Kocher

after storying-with the spring-fed source of Birrarung Marr (2005—2022)

Enter by river
mouth agape, black
stubble on your cloven feet:
soon your animal soul's a skirling.
Breath pursued by whistling teeth.

Knee-jerk. Distaste. Clockless
waiting: the listless dead stacked
on high, no wind in the canning
factory. Your snoring elongates.
Flock from box to spectre, desolate.

I nudge your ribs, you mumble,
fling your arm across my face
& tattoo thick Hey-ho! the
upward clutter of an elevator,
storm-lit snapping beaks.

I haul my nest against your back
warm-buried, strapped with wax
& redneck locks, I wrack
my limbs doldrum steep, dive
the sandbags, shred concrete.

⁂

With the eyes of seals and the tongues of lions,
fickle cunt take comfort in the draped and sleeping cat.

The ocean is weaving its wild fennel,
the floating heron, the swamp-like calm in the nuclear ditch.

(Not only could I see but touch him, passing through the happenings
like a whistle or a wraith, and on this day of hellfire how to know

which way to leap? Because desire is full of endless distances,
O little pumpkinseed, I remember too much. It is said

cats have nine lives and I assure you I am the least
difficult of men—how not more so, now I am dead?

(It is true I knew nothing of Love or its dealings
which is why I lived so well in my shell among the powerful

and crazed. Do not upbraid me, Daughter.
Mine was a hollowed walnut, no sweetmeat to give.

Still, I would that I could, had I had it. Yet I entreat you,
look at my sleek reflection in the hospital glass.

A full head of hair, shining silver.
Admire my locks.

Muscled-up mosquitoes rev the furry ground light.

Murder-slick, they pierce through leather to sup
on the same juicy stream beneath our skin
as that which skids us through mist:

thudding kingfisher notes on braided grass country:
groundwater slips the roots of a vascular
apple tree strewn with blackberry so thick,

the mozzies that prick and suck seem mild
compared to the water that burns
our ankles soon bearded in blood.

⁂

Well yes, tiger snakes *do* inhabit both living banks.
Slashed blackberry stumps—*Look out!*—still sting the unwary.
Two *diama bicolour* or blue bottle ants lace your foot,

the creek a thin trickle, melodious. No bite.
Silence.   Its bridgework hardly a choice, but hard
to break. Sometimes, sheer futility absorbs the damsel-

fly stuck shimmering inside an orb spider's wheel
like lard. Sardonic, we *could* rotate the circumstantial—
but *Leave it,* you say.   Later, you turn back, taxidermal.

⁂

I want to see out, this trick I fall back on   broom, rag, bucket
to peer inside our own lives   we have to scrub   a bewildering assortment of old

disciplines worn like silk   worm mouths to thread   & wherever did this pink
amaryllis come from   naked belladonna   stems

she never knew   how surprisingly she sparkles in the dark   well trained you are
d(r)ear daily scaling   of course we never liked   being scraped & knocked

or caught in the mucky grooves   the sliding panes   slide upon   I
never asked   so much glass   we are asking now

the name that means   a longed-for monotreme
never mind how long the shining lasts   it feels good to have done nothing but

make watertight   the ground light   rimed in river silt
drying on the steps beside the cloth   clairtangent through and through

deadlight blisters write prescriptions in glass

Nathan Shepherdson

do we complete silence when we speak.

pull nails out of wood by breathing in.

did our prayers
get caught in the crevice
of the left elbow

never made it
to the hands

can we curse
the inefficient sleep
in sunlight

anchors in bassinets
sink us all to birth

the skin always the first reserve for writing paper,
onion-tunic-crinkle in its envelope fenced with UK colour,
Riley endorsed, still in the air after forty years, still hoping
to be offered consciousness or accommodation
between the floorboards of an equals sign,
poste restante pillow plumped
and waiting,

vision hiking through its oval window
clocks a half-second flash across the valley,
a blade, never tested, remembers
the address of its favourite
vein,

as a boy ←
the crazy dentist in the village
showed you x-rays of common words
lodged between the teeth
of uncommon animals

& ←

you understood
what was said
by not saying it

hid your lips beneath your tongue
without telling yourself
where they were

THIS →

as a pre-bruxist manoeuvre
until your jaw pops its rivets
to open like the spoonbill bow
of a Higgins boat, where you get
to step ashore, onto yourself ←

the classified ads for memory are not answered.

soprano-shakedown of the spine into fish frames.

St Peter mending his nets
sews his fingers
together,

you tell me,

‘how you lose everything
when you find out
why you’re here’

you tell me,

how you used to watch
young conductors as shadows
draw lines in salt-air, baton count
in an emphysemic symphony
that refuses to end, to end,
inside twilit stones
on a Sussex shore

again,

this is not to say
what is not to be
said

the ribs the first obstacle course
for breathing in shallow graves
chalk bells are buried
with their ears
inside them,

mechanical brows on pilfered wind
measure lone tides in Salter-scale ratios
into your wife’s departed eyes

the enamel on her teeth
given a permanent home
under loose skin on the apple
that exists more than once
to exist less than ever

no less than less, a comet
in a paper bag catches fire
when it's ready,

lies to the flesh in the fruit bowl
about when it'll be
(back)

because an abacus built for touch
can only count
(back)

rooms continue to polish bones
with(i)n) walls
with)o(ut(us

'all i ask you to avoid
is prefacing any drawing
with a specific line.'[i]

all i ask is that you honour
the recurring dream of a white collar
waiting for its leash to snake-charm
up, from muddy ground, to attach itself
without being
noticed

through hairline cracks in blue agate, you witness
the power imbalance as you take two selves for a walk,
twin shadows effervesce gossip as to your whereabouts,
as to your future, as they slip notes under the door
of the philosopher-spy, which say things
like, 'he keeps light in the freezer', or,
'he's just stirred two years gone, one

year at a time, into black tea'

butterknife crease at the elision point in new breath.

carsick theories always pull over on the same road.

Phyllis taught you
to cut a loaf of bread
with a look

to leave the knives
in the returns box at the neolithic library
for assassins and butchers

brains should be allowed to pack their own parachutes.

the colours that never end are the colours that never begin.

(and they're all at your disposal)

each one on its roulette wheel
serves every patient corpuscle
in infinity

soap-carved thoughts
wash what is not
there

as kitchen wisdom, as a half-joke
in a whole sentence, our grandmothers
would have said,

'you should only steal time
if you're going to sell it
(back) to yourself'

it's no surprise that trees have paper skulls is it.

rain inside the head falls up.

the sting in the meadow
a hoof's delight to crush
a farmer's cruel neck

this blockade of fingernails
forces you to watch
one thing →

to yell yourself at blind questions
that persist in being
half-mast

at least booksellers are animals in our laps
who pay circus fleas to jump inside full stops
now roaming free range along our margins

because there's no walking home from eternity.

bridges perspire the feet that walk over them.

with paws dipped in Indian ink, a poodle trio
shuffled under giant coconut cups
on a timber floor bark time
in time at time on time
as time so time is time
until their magician
can no longer
hear them

the last canine episode of *The Three Stooges*

ran for eight weeks, worn teeth as loyalty badges,
dutifully handed in, before one by one,
they buried themselves
in the back garden

small dapple-grey bodies
now readied for the hemispheric overflow
between the Bremer and the Orwell
in Ipswich

silence learned
how to ride horses
at an early age

no body was rhetoric until it said something.

our bodies were not rhetoric until we said no.

chaff-rustle of truth
from three braided heads
of garlic

music lobbies evolution
that ears be allowed
to blink

( ) (   )

( ) (   )

is this the eyelid ←
you'll use to snuff
the last match

morphine rain

seduced by the slow dance
on a marble mattress

‘it is a decoy,

just as an occasion
is not an origin
and neither one
is the object.’[ii]

‘\/ \/ \ /////,

//// \/ \\ ///\/\/\
\/ \// \\ //\/\\
\\/ \/\//// /\/
\/ /// //////.’

don’t forget,

,

you need to sculpt legs
for these martlets
before you leave,

,

[i] Letter from Mrs. Valerie Eliot to (_ _) 2nd December 1982.

[ii] Letter from J.H. Prynne to (_ _) 3rd April 1999.

A Series of Sepia Photos Discovered in the Garage

Glenn McPherson

1

Three streets over the most beautiful
Worlds begin. Little idea what
The Buddhists call them, they are busy removing

Hair by sword: in Laos, you can wake
And provide for them a daily portion of rice
Or dried fish at dawn.

2

There is a frog tumbling pebbles.

3

                                        Yesterday's
Paper from an emptied paint tin reads itself in the ash
Between a handful of twigs lit by Socrates

As the last eternal hour of night performs
Dawn.

4

          When the devil shows up at heaven
The drinking games start. It isn't long

Before he falls to bragging. Two dice
For a friendly game of Street Craps. Beneath
White electrical cord a naked bulb burns

With interrogation. Wild eyes, wild eyes—he will
Curse you and die before dawn.

5

Twelve tombs
Protected by twelve kings belonging to Sari Saltuk

Are bound in a series of sepia photos in the garage
Of Ajnur like a stack of cards.

6

Out of water
High in the Balkans, bears speak to wolves

Bringing dawn.

7

If it is up to us to never want
To come back, where should we start?
The city is too light at all times to encourage

The kind of dancing required.
How can we expect desire to lift
The dandelion at dawn?

8

Others: O yes of course,
Others are the simple gait of the beggar
In the body of ants

Feeding along the crimson line
Who will never sleep with anyone's wife
Because he is married to dawn.

9

Well, every world

It is like that, even at night in the hot
Country where, hung to dry on scrap
Iron remains of a light-plane,

Work shirts remind men they are not
Related and this is no pentecost,
It is almost dawn.

10
Be the quiet pigeon.

See how it waits above the square
Drawn by the call to proceed in humility,
For that is its colour. Each window sill

Is a ladder rung. Find without
Sweetness the wearied prayer. Sit
In darkness, it will be dawn soon.

11

We become agriculture. Stiff, arthritic corn.
Our fortress, the food plain. We ramify and are
Ramifications of the first wounds to arrive

On a full moon in August
From the bones of a fig tree
Giving licence to a new dawn

An idea bred among the ruins
Of Molech.

12

On hard, bitter-cold nights, a blood-
Lamb can think through rock. Without scotch
It may die come dawn.

13

Moths
Hold too much magic. They watch as silver
Dust settle inside the room where a drug

Is administered to help his wife sleep. In four
Hours he will change her position, press
With a cool hand her forehead, sing

In a whisper, Norwegian Wood, weep
When he makes dawn. Afterward,
Wake up. What else is there

To do. It is as if Tamar, before being
Dragged off, kissed, placed the ring and the stick
By our bed, the thread moving away from the dawn.

the experience economy

David Stavanger

[Giving birth is a destination. Like a fair. Authorities are considering an admission fee before a couple even sets foot in pre-conception. At 'pre-contemplation'. Before the development of mechanical attractions. Charges for the ride—the carnival of carnal thought—remain free. Parents would then be forced to stage a much better experience to attract guests, eagerly anticipating the start of the sensory festivities.]

[A combination of goods or services is needed. Sometimes the child requires immediate assembly, a time of teamwork and technical thrills. Other times they arrive via unpaid labour, the sweatshop of legacy and lust. This is what we call a productivity miracle. Placentas can be stored in an ice box to be re-gifted or on-sold as a luxury purse. This is one way we build close bonds with reproductive capitalism.]

[Our labour experience is a perfect example—you're paying for so much more than a newborn. You're paying for the cosy ambiance. You're paying for skilled friendly staff, a superior birthing suite, a supportive cast of characters to spectate the big event online. The sensation of desire as existential demand, delivery as constant supply. The parent that gets recorded first on official record is considered the 'primary carer'. You can't copyright a face; some material is born into the public domain.]

[The first-born is often a non-fungible commodity. Facile sentimentality is the secret weapon of serial conception: one is often insufficient to trade, while two or more can form part of a set. They say the second one is easier. Like saying the problem with water is that it breaks. The spectrum of choice is endless, from bath to bed to Uber, squatting in a space shuttle, an uncut umbilical cord unspooling through money and time.]

[The value of the transformation: they will soon have your eyes and consumer confidence. Walk down the compliment tunnel together: becoming patient too quickly (*applause*), less consistent at night and more critical of morning (*muted claps*), monitoring a child's whereabouts with an electronic device in the shape of an ankle (*rewards*). Now is the time to relax, go to a nice restaurant and eat real food as a real couple, knowing where every item is on this menu.]

[An experience cannot lack the spontaneity of life: a nappy full of sudden sorrow; the discovery of back vomit; a bird hitting a window; walking in on your partner rearranging themself, deep in the consumption phenomena of pornographic daydream. While external problems may cause internal frustrations, we must offer fascinating displays of family, peacocks within the mundane. Needing ever more hardcore material is evident.]

[Pre-programmed experiences are pre-packaged and on-brand. Catchy slogans stick: *no kids are the new kids*. Tick. The child is just a prop for what's known as 'parentertainment'. A big screen shows a mother breastfeeding a clone. The playground swing breaks. A cafe opens down the road based on make-believe. Parents gather there child-free (but remain parents), talk about the joys of resentment-free raising, order empty cups of coffee and blank plates, paying for the magic state of gathering in our simulated connection environment.]

[Buyers of experiences are what Walt Disney termed 'guests'. Best guests attend kids' parties where parents neither make the birthday cake nor throw the princess-themed party. It's not even held at their home, an amorphous construct. The key to this business is staging a memorable event for the kids-in-us-all, whilst discreetly showcasing that ninety-percent of people with certified social mobility have self-confidence in turning children into stars. Mickey Mouse started out as a rabbit.]

[The provision of psychic gratification: divesting from dad, seeking better qualities of wife, the screened life immaculate, lying in bed with a lover now durational sleep companion. Parenting has only encountered trouble because we have failed to refresh our experiences, dethroned by the more traditional capacity of 'outcome' such as staying together and checking weekend weather apps. Our projected outlook will extend AI-fuelled family accessories, the interface with a surrogate life.]

[Parenting requires active participation. Name the child after another child or on-trend object, drive in an approved SUV, oversee endless summer sports, engage in engaged storytelling and intergenerational myth-making. If you're a venture capitalist, read an infant *Dune* at bedtime. If you're a stay-at-home parent, show them cavalier pictures of your cavoodle on Instagram. It's important to respect and preserve all forms of life, not unlike a modern CEO. Tell your child you are not like your parents. Services to your child will be intangible and occasionally memorable. A shared calendar with coloured squares will remind you who you planned to love.]

If I hold out my hand

Emilie Collyer

As light fades I stand cold-hipped, outside
this cluster of demountables, holiday
digs on an agistment farm. It is bleak,
pretty, Lara Plains. We two are here
to heal part of what has broken. A Horse
strolls over. Hoofs, cloud, dirt, his breath

velvet. I want to touch him but his head
is so big. My sister visited a cousin's
farm once and was kicked. Adrienne Rich
writes about how the word love is threaded
with violence. Horse snorts and lopes away.
Stubby-legged Men in hi-vis the next hut over

clutching coldies, approach Horse with ease,
pat and feed him until the gloaming is done.
I have only lived Horses through story. I cried
when Phar Lap galloped to victory, wounded
hoof spurting blood. 'It's the size of his heart!'
the Men all said, how he would never give up.

My boyfriend laughs at how envious I am
of the hi-vis Men. Not cruelly. We watch
Eurovision. It is the year Ukraine is favourite.
It is the year Ukraine wins. Mostly because
of the war but the song is also quite good.
We don't talk about the thing we are healing.

Black sky floods the world outside. In
The Godfather they warned a Man
by putting a severed Horse head in his bed.
You'd know the wail, mournful trumpet

refrain, even if you don't know the movie.
Even if you haven't seen the gold silk sheets

soaked in blood, the Man waking. Screaming.
Wind rattles our hut through the night,
Doppler moan of trucks a restless lullaby.
Our neighbour, whose Men-friends in their sixties
keep having heart surgeries, has told us
eighty percent of open-heart recipients

regret the operation. They end up maudlin,
drifting and death wishing, something
about the separation: often the hearts are alone,
outside the body for six hours, the rehousing
an unbearable grief. Phar Lap's pickled heart
is on display in a jar thousands of miles away

from his taxidermy body. I wake to car doors
banging, teenage Boys from other huts
jostled out of bed. I peer out. Hoodies and shorts,
trotting through mist, hurried along
by the bark of a Man, colts loaded
onto the back of a truck. I have no reason

to worry about these Boys I don't know
but their legs are so bare and the Man's voice
so loud. Across the field, Horses are standing,
sleeping. I was not a Horse Girl but the eros
of that Boy in *Equus*, blinding the Horses,
his urge to be seen and not seen,

the thrill of our carnality, lodged like a burr.
Maybe young Girls adore Horses to feel
thunder in their bodies that their mouths
are disallowed. My first orgasm
low brick fence childhood home,
by accident with my first boyfriend.

The partner who said straight up
he didn't 'do' oral sex. The lover I asked
to chafe my nipples to the edge of pain.
I know what you mean, Adrienne. The way
fake fur makes my throat itch. The way
there are no scissors in this thin walled

unit so we slit our two-minute noodle
sachets open with a blunt paring knife.
The way the clock radio by the bed
is set to Triple M and DJ Dave Gleeson
from the Screaming Jets laments,
how disappointed he was back when

Alanis Morrisette and Ryan Reynolds
split up. We are not splitting.
We will not disappoint DJ Dave.
After the gravel settles, after the sky
relents its attachment to what can't be seen,
I sit on the deck, dip a teabag into a mug.

My boyfriend will not wake for a while.
We are different clocks. Magpies
announce morning proper. I could run.
Two clicks along the road and back,
sucking in silver country air. My Achilles
is tender; mornings have a limping

stagger. I like the gym trainers. They
say keep running. They say impact
builds cartilage. They say don't avoid
the bitumen. Mostly, I know,
they kill a Horse that breaks its leg.
Light bones and heavy body make

recovery rare. Their lives in our
clumsy hands. Oh Love!
How to treat a body not our own.
I wait. We can walk, instead,
together, once the day warms,
careful footfall, our arms tentative,

our skin brushing. I hope Horse
will visit again, give me a slow blink
second chance. I have found small
packets of sugar. Not cubes, but still.
Books always talk about how their
soft lips tickle the skin of your hand.

Fishbone Ferns

B. R. Dionysius

the fishbone ferns tunnel ball over
the treated pine log that I stole from
next door. they form a sawtooth arch.

my son was an accomplice as I hoisted
the greasy poles over our fence like a
late entry highland games athlete.

don't be concerned. it's a rental. the logs
twelve in all, were decommissioned years
ago & bound up by lamb's tail vine.

we took rocks too, half buried boulders
that had long fallen out of shape as border
material; crooked teeth parents could never

afford to correct. the cannonball-sized ones
thumped onto our lawn as we shot-putted
them: a distant wallop of mortar rounds.

the treated wood & granite stones were
put to work again as border guards, but
the ferns don't care. their natural arch

gives them grace. we walk. on the oven
top footpath black ants finish flensing
the carcass of the noisy minor chick.

its flesh is gone. scrapped, anything
of wealth stripped from its olive hull
by these insect gleaners who comb

the day-old wreck, relentless as tide.
it looks like the blueprint for a bird
laid out on that blue-black greasy paper.

only one prototype was built &
it didn't enter mass production.
days later & the body's vanished

nature's crime scene cleaners efficient.
we always seem to stop at the dead things
to examine, to contemplate final throes

death bends like a piece of cardboard
& is just as flimsy. anyone could do entropy.
just sit back & let decay do all the work.

*

the electricity towers kill us like a slow
release poison. you live too near to them
& you'll go sterile, or develop cancer.

the towers are fitted with barbed wire
chokers to stop hands from reaching up.
silk from a cyborg spider's spinneret.

they are their own ashram. they are still,
they hum in unison, their steel spines
imposing as a border chain-link fence.

*

now they also say the torresian crows
have evolved, nesting in man-made
buildings & ledges as never before.

distancing themselves from unpredictable
trees, who obey the wind like a broken
confessor. thunderstorms will do that.

help you adapt. in our backyard the crow
parents teach their two young to dip bread
into the birdbath to soften it. biscuits in tea.

when I come into the kitchen they all
flinch, then pause. they hunch their black
shoulders & cock eyes as if expecting a blow.
they know which houses are safe,
structures that don't move like a branch
in high winds. their next generations

will grow up not understanding what
trees are for. just another obstacle to
check their lift against, to avoid like us.

I clean the algae out for them. it must
feel like scraping blubber from whale
hide. it is a wet intelligence they possess.

*

they are discussing eco poetry in inner
city melbourne. the anthropocene. big
ideas with little words growing inside.

one keeps their books in a himalayan pouch.
another, a cow leather satchel. the third writes
in a cadmium script on their iPhone.

they have coopted a genre they have never
lived. they once grew up on a farm, but now
exist in exile. summonses don't stretch north.

*

there is cooperation everywhere but here.
a young galah is taught to wet its whistle
from the park's dog trough by its parent.

we stop & watch. the fledgling is a paler pink
than its mother or father. it whinges away
like a good child, but follows when they fly.

it lands on the tower that sounds like insects
run through its spiny cable. it is unaware of
the carcinogenic qualities of this no fly zone.

on farms they are still gunned down I tell my
son, by farmers who don't want their panicum
crops decimated. or they cut down all their trees

to stop the parrots from nesting, from gaining
a foothold, a HQ to plan their next assault. I
prosthelytize it's like cutting off a ghetto's water

supply or electricity to force a stateless people
to go away. whoever has a stronger will to power
will endure. bust always follows the boom.

it can be quite WW1, out on the downs, bodies
hung up in barbed wire, left to rot as a sign to
others—don't try it, don't cross into no man's.

*

eastern greys watch us as we walk. it has been
burned into their racial memory, that we are
predator x, the apex killer of our fiery epoch.

their ears unfold intricately like a handkerchief
or a small satellite dish. they measure distance
between us & their elephant grass escape.

the males wait to receive medals. pouches
bulge with frenetic pace as juveniles take
advantage of their marsupial isolation cell.

some days the mob will stand at salute, or
if spooked, bound into the tall grass to be
aloof from walkers in cooperative distrust.

*

the brisbane river's brown chest cavity
rises at dusk as it draws in its huge tidal
breath. mangroves set their bollard roots.

we stop at the dying tree, ten metres tall
its trunk & limbs riddled with holes as though
caught up in a thompson gun shoot-out.

so many rounds of borer entry wounds,
an overkill like bonnie & clyde peppered
by the fbi. its grey bark torn suit cloth.

a fringe of leaves cling onto life, but my
son points out the lost cause, the slow rot
now home to geckos who gain vengeance.

*

on the treated pine council fence, two tawny
frogmouths perch four metres apart, siblings
or a mated pair is lost as night hunts down

the last light. they hiss, not at us but to each
other, a signal to take flight, to soar through
the spiny obstacle course of casuarinas

& begin their night fighter terror, whiskers
sharp as radar antenna locating their prey.
each afternoon we look for the camouflaged

airfield of their nest, but nothing gives it away.
they are stealth, dull greys & blacks reflecting
no moonlight; strong armament of beak & claw.

*

I give my brother in law some fishbone
ferns to fill a bald spot. he tears them away
like hair from a scalp in a fight; rhizomes

resist to the end. the filigree of fine roots
dug out, sounding like thin paper tearing.
the stony soil knocking like marbles.

they will thrive in his yard, these plants
whose leaves I used to strip from their stems
as a child, no thought to the irreparable

damage; being thrilled by the finger touch
of the alternate leaves as they shredded like
rotten ladder steps collapsing under me.

I neither like nor dislike them. they have
found their niche in my garden & clever,
replicated themselves in another space.

my son grabs the fronds now & shreds them
like in those old cartoons when a fish goes in
a mouth all flesh, then comes out a skeleton.

Falling, falling

Jo Gardiner

Fifty years ago, a young student, off to see a film,
in a mistyped moment, mis-stepped in the dark,
down a flight of steps—like hard rainfall, silent
as snowfall, about as soft as icefall. With all sails

flapping in the wind like broken wings, an ankle
snapped and now, after decades of arthritis
like root rot, you're in the hospital, and the night
says—in a voice that's just another code

you'll never crack—*Expect me soon.* You memorise
a face to take down this dark-mouthed rabbit
hole, but the space between you grows too fast.
Outside the theatre, the anaesthetist is a wreck.

To calm him, you tell the story of the double-jointed
child who broke the laws of gravity, the ether
pillow pressed hard into her face to knock her out.
Now, beyond his head, in the theatre,

stage lights show a human leg dangling from a hook
and you hear a saw. A nurse spots you staring
and slams the door and says *It is our wounds that open
us to the world, and in our scar's the balm of nature.*

*

Morning, and the surgeon stands tall at the foot
of the bed where you lie, a new ankle sewn
inside your foot. He wears fine leather shoes, no socks.
Above him six wild white geese on the fly.

Inside the cast, the foot belongs to someone else:
    plastic and filigreed metal housed inside—
toggled and looped, braided and anchored through
    tissue to drilled-down bone. All tied off with a jugger

knot by the surgeon with no socks. My love sits in the chair
    by my bed, but I'm bent over a broom
sweeping ginkgo leaves fanned flat on our garden path
    by rain. He is present when I wake and sits

with me till late as my mother sat under our roof
    of rain on the cold edge of the Strait.
In my fever dreams, she was ever there, her hand
    a cool spell on my head. She'd lift me

from tangled sheets, remake the bed, bathe me
    with a warm rough flannel, dry my limbs
and fold me back into the sound of rain.
Measuring her love—like weighing honey.

*

In hospital, you drift out each night and stalk the dark
    wards. You dream of falling, falling. Each step
you take holds a slow disclosure of the truth. On heavy
    meds, you see through smoke and mirrors:

each moment of your life's stitched into your body
    by the pointillist. At night, you wave a hand
across the score scrawled on the white pillow:
    a bone flute plays you songs, and you remember

how, following your lust for flight, hanging once
    in fear from a parachute above a boat
on a lake. Lightly tethered as a spider to its thread,
    you stepped from clouds into a cobalt windfall.

*

Home and everything falls out of its time
    and it's the nights you travel. Shackled to them,
your wounded body hungers for shadows.
    You wake just as Venus becomes visible,

and dusk flows across the valley and home to roost.
    The red bedside lamp throws shadows
about the room piled with books. As the days reach
    further, you finally can sleep at night again

and hear a sledgehammer strike a piece of metal.
    Each blow rings out clear and sure. Then again.
Not a beat is missed. From inside your own long
    coffin, you hear them hammer every nail.

*

To a wide stretch of morning, your love opens
    the window. Overnight, the house has held
the heat, and now it catches streams of cool air
    that start a conversation with your pale face.

A butcher bird's voice travels through box gums
    —her notes come in limpid drops
and leave you hostage to her song that flies
    across the memory plain where pain

once grew in nervy spikes. It seems to have passed
    now but when are we ever really unlatched
from danger? In the reflection on the glass table,
    birds fly upside down. You wheel out onto the deck

and let sunlight touch your body. Hair falls from
    your head across your hand: the soft horror

of torn cobwebs on the skin. The breeze lifts
    bedsheets draped in sun. In a long wall,

the dogwood and cherry enclose you in their green
    arms. A storm comes and afternoon pours
through rain into the yellow room. Everything glows:
    the bedsheets, the socks in the basket, a purple

cotton jumper. Your white face in the wardrobe
    mirror. Through the trees, a sleeve of blue.
You leave the bed to try to walk on crutches. Down
    in the humid garden, a lyrebird shrieks.

*

A burning numbness. Toes of ice. A crisp-
    skinned lump at the bottom of a leg,
membranes splodged with suture wounds.
    The foot is like a child who knows

she's not wanted, who's left to wander behind
    the others, or forgotten in the car
when everyone else has gone inside for tea.
    You tell yourself one day this foot

will walk again. Four weeks in, you don't believe
    it. You have no proof. With its long history
of falling, the truth lies in a cryptic mirror:
    and all you see ahead is uncertainty.

*

Memory's a door key dropped in the dark:
    you can't remember what it was like to walk—
the flight and spin of feet, the pivot and turn
    when you went each day to see the glossies

mob the sheoak seeds. No need of feet, their flight
scorned you even then. Caged here now
you hear them in the distance, and find
a truant feather they've left to taunt.

*

It's *Act II*, and déjà vu is the patient on the table,
green boned and unsure. Sucking on Endone
and sinking under, you flinch as they split the foot
again, the one that once walked across

the Roman hills and along the Appian Way
on summer nights and chased the long,
golden limbs of Italian light. As you think of bones
dug up in Pompeii and closely examined

for signs of infection, the same boyish surgeon—
wanton with blood and blade—
shreds your leaf-thin skin into a bucket by the bed.
An unknown man sobs in another room.

*

At home again, your bones grow thin as dragonfly
wings. The night winds rattle through them
where they lie in moist earth below the pond
and the waterlily spreads her green hands

over swimming koi—sleek orange blossoms
who appear and disappear like slow breath
and listen to the great silence when it comes
to tell you what you already know.

The Luck Dragon

Scott-Patrick Mitchell

after the journal logs of the 2015 Perth Canyon expedition aboard the research vessel Falkor and The Neverending Story

Prelude

To anchor is to bob in one spot, but where is the fun in that: descend through a lens. Above, cinematic semantics add texture, the way pressure pushes water on, up, around. Below, the no-thing of not-knowing waiting to be found. Blue, stretching across a map, shades velvet wet. Salt laps the hull, eager to swallow.

February 20

On land, a group of scientists are preparing for a quest. Down there, a canyon. They pack with improvisation, know saltwater can corrupt. They cleanse test tubes in preparation, using a furnace marked:

THIS IS NOT AN OVEN.

On the small floating island of their research ship, malfunction will be an axiom. Pyjamas and Ugg boots, the comfort of home. Somebody packs *Twenty Thousand Leagues Under The Sea* for the irony. Speculation is shared between them. From afar, the luck dragon swims toward shore.

February 26

What is science if not a never-ending story. In the movie, Falkor carries Atreyu across a green screen as The Nothing consumes Fantasia. Here, the narrative is reversed: the unknown is filled in across a bank of monitors contained in the research vessel. Nothing becomes something, is quantified. Scientists within a bastion of machinery and notes. They shall name all that they see. Some take Dramamine or ginger to soothe the sickness of swell. Others look to the line of the horizon. One hundred years ago, such an expedition would have been cramped and stowed, but *Falkor* has luck sewn into his hull. Buoyed with knowledge. In the galley, a sign reads:

THIS IS AN OVEN.

From it, the lull of fresh bread. In the scales of this, a stream of ones and zeros transmogrify. The dragon is never alone on the high sea: the scientists feed it baked goods, their dreams. But not all at once. They still have far to go.

March 2

Split day into light and dark. Each part plays a role. Sun glow: cast a rosette into the rough.

It is a complexity for measuring complexity.

Conductivity,
temperature, depth: such things un-abstract to create an image painted from data-sets. They measure salinity, arrange sampling bottles on a metal frame.

One thousand metres, descend into new realm.

During the night,
sonar sweeps the pitch to create bathymetric maps. An inversion of the unseen, shaded into orange and red and green:

details become apparent.

March 5

Lophelia engineers a habitat.
Small mechanisms aqua form.
In dimensions of three,
invertebrates transform barren into sea garden.
Everything is Antipodean. Coral is used
to the cold, lack of light, knows how to make a skeleton
for itself in the harsh chemical composition.
They learn to manipulate currents,
but in doing so, grow slow.
No photosynthetic algae to meal.
Instead, the water columns provide zooplankton.
This is a refuge: these souls learn to adapt,
but the crisis above may still reach them
as cystographic waves engulf the sun,
draw heat
sinking.

March 6

A Remotely Operated Underwater vehicle is called ROV for short.
As in: rover of the aqua pastoral, roving beneath tide.
Small mechanical mammal become eyes for those who stay dry.
Little robot who can,
withstand the fathom.
It dives, finds sea crabs pincered to a cliff,
passes purple sea cucumbers,
feather star,
urchins.
Bioluminescence in the ether of ink.
A seahorse, not-drowning
in the swamp of this.
Up on deck, the scientists lean in,
marvel at the fantastical written across pixels.

March 7 – 9

One mile down.
Venus flytrap anemones
close their arms
around that which they love. To eat,
nematocysts helps prey pass on, away.
Elsewhere, a Brisingid sea star lifts
as if Velcro off the seafloor to devour.
Fragile, they are dubbed armless
for the way the fall apart
when dredged in net.
Golden coral metallic stygian
while a basket star tangles limbs into drink.
Mushroom soft coral
glow in the light of the ROV.
Further in, glass sponges
spin skeletons from silica,
a home for a pair of mating shrimp,
imprisoned in a white saltlike prism.
A symphony of otherness.
The researchers observe,

dream of salt and brine,
an inverse sky,
darkening.

March 10

Canyon: connect shallow shelves to a deep basin.
Create heat, as in a hotspot.
As in, come sea-life, find this place,
find the warmth you need
to feed and breed.
Migration is a sea shanty,
singing you home,
a call and response passed on.
How The Leeuwin Current
tugs tropical water along the coast.
Beneath, a stream
of food and fauna flow.
Along wall, eddies.
Nutrients upwell into sunlit zone.
This, a dinner bell.
Aggregations with open mouths
summoned:
they wolf
with
such
small hunger.

March 12

Moonchild

open your hand

there

a single grain of sand

a drop of seawater

a canyon.

Make a wish

it will be as if

the nothing

never-was.

Epilogue

Specimens are packed up, noted. *Falkor* turns around, faces land. The expedition ends. In laboratories and behind desks, the scientists begin a complex cartography that articulates expanse, adds contrast to the map. Findings will find each other. A clear picture will appear. Sometime later, photographs from this adventure will be published in the pages a glossy scientific magazine. A poet will buy a copy at a second-hand bookstore, be inspired by what exists just beyond their front door.

Years after that,

this poem

will wash up

in your mouth

.

crechaid

Dan Disney

fleeing poverty in famine-stricken Co. Cork, on 23rd April 1828 attempted to steal 28 yards of cotton from a shop in London's 'Battle Bridge' (now known as Kings Cross). Apprehended, she was charged (larceny) & sent to trial on 29th May. Sentenced to 7 years in Van Diemen's Land, was transported together with her 3 sons & almost 100 other female prisoners on the 'Harmony', sailing from Woolwich on 13th September. 17 weeks later, the ship arrived in VDL. Her sons, Charles (9), William (5), & Joseph (4) were removed from her, & placed into what was then known as the *King's Orphan Asylum.* was one of the first prisoners transported by the British empire to enter the *Cascades Female Factory* (built 1828).

14th January, 1829

what was it doing that day, the
weather, your heart
bobbing at the larcenous
VDL coves, did the sun
squat bright in the clink
of leg-ironed air, & did
uniforms, bark-mouthed, uniformly
leer that day the HARMONY
cast a 5-score slew, & does
air bend forth like a gent's knee
at your back, & when
your padlocked sons are removed
(peeled as if skinship
fit for orphanage flayings, then

lutruwita was referred to by colonizers as 'Van Diemen's Land' until another exonym, 'Tasmania,' was codified (01.01.1856)

***

THE FEMALE FACTORY AND HOUSE OF CORRECTION

We most sincerely congratulate the Public upon the opening of that most important establishment of punishment, for the disorderly branches of the female prisoner population, and which we are led to believe is intended to be equally subservient to the checking of the growing depravity of the free female population, as a House of Correction. Since the opening of the Institution, the fair disobedients awarded to its accommodation as a recess to their wild and disorderly propensities, most anxiously crave a dispensation of its benefits.

Colonial Times, Friday 30 January 1829, pp. 3)

***

what does it do, Ur-mother,
heart in the weathering
step of your otherworld scowl
into the muds of a self, wrenched
by garrisoned gowls — an unpleasant person
nosing rifle-sight fields, did — (Irish Gaelic; pejorative)
you think
to yourself, *which outlandish*
hell is this, o what
across the heart-ripped
day were your meteorologies (no,
ask instead this: *was it not best*
not to feel at all)

***

& what next, the interlocking
days not
like a clasp of son hands
gone to *goodness*
knows, cycle of men & moons
in foul weather
working bad weathers
into unmagically foul men
& never a *fearadh na fáilte* — a pouring-out of welcome
on the constabularily smeared — (Irish Gaelic)
faces pocking the blur, brutes
ranked in shot
nerves, grandmother, *how*
did you live in your mind, force into your heart
the emptinesses, sharply

***

COURT REPORTING

The Criminal Sessions at Launceston closed on Monday last, where the awful sentence of death was passed on no less that eighteen criminals, viz. 7 for sheep-stealing, 3 for cattle-stealing, 1 for a rape, and the rest for burglary. His Honor, the Chief Justice PEDDER was much affected while passing sentence on the prisoners.

(*Colonial Times*, Friday 30 January 1829, pp. 3)

***

from the fug of your peatbog
mind & hemispherically
turned, grandmother, what
could you make
of the lynchings, gunsmoke, the
guards & the ladies
planting bodies
into stippled & sunbroken grounds
declaimed in an Englishing
noise, & what
was whitely becoming
thinkable now, in the bone midsts
of a misty & militant phonics,
your fist-hearted
masters chitchatting, under bonnets
& the droll regalias
doffing unwithering smiles

between 1804 and 1853, approximately 76,000 convicts were sent to VDL . . . while the number of Indigenous people killed in the same period remains a contested figure, credible historians deem the murderous dispossessions that took place on *lutruwita* as genocide

***

payriminpatatik '~~Greenes Point~~' luyntim '~~Pavement Point~~' mayntranga '~~Detention River~~' mutawaynatji '~~Emu Point~~' lukukina '~~Archers Point~~' wukalina '~~Mt. William~~' punalatina 'Mt. Cameron' minamata '~~Lake Youl~~' kunawi '~~Lake Leake~~' mayaluwarana '~~Schouten Island~~' tukana 'Tasman Peninsula' putalina '~~Oyster Cove~~' lunawuni '~~Bruny Island~~' laylatiya '~~Recherche Bay~~' taluna '~~Huon River~~' wirarawn '~~Hobbs Island~~'

***

if you're desperate, & you are
told endlessly how *you're good*
for only one thing, Hobarton as
the spill & churn

of horizontal abyss, *bean si,* — netherworldly woman (Irish Gaelic)
nil a saol ach ceo, bodies — this world is nothing but mist (Irish Gaelic)
transplanting empire across
transactional sludge-rutted streets,
patterns through a dawning
epochal noise, in each
wrongheaded guv'nor
gaoler squatter free
settler & sailor, in each lady &
whipped horse or inmate
sent to the Interior, which — any part of VDL outside the two main centres
syntaxes to make eyes unsee — (Hobarton, Launceston)
unholiness as divine
bestowal . . . in your Gaelic
the word will be
crechaid (vb. to plunder, spoil
or ravage but also mark & sear,
cauterize), settlement
as smoke-blinded swarming (unsacrosanct)
one slaughter after the next

***

CHIT CHAT

It has reached us by a settler, that Boomer, the black native, having struck the Serjeant of the detachment, to which he was acting as guide, in pursuit of the Aboriginies, endeavored to escape, and received the merited reward of his treachery and presumption by being shot dead. So much for reliance upon the fidelity of a native!

(*Colonial Times,* Friday 30 January 1829, pp. 3)

***

'& you'll hear it again just fine, yer Sasanach, — a person from England (Irish Gaelic; pejorative)
gabh suas . . .' — fuck yourself (Irish Gaelic)

***

inside, again, hard labour
in their factory hovel,
the lye-stink of Matronly
dryheaving rules, convecting
the Wash Tub &
snarling in steam, you are

Crime Class (again)
& amok, they say, but what today
of Charlie, Bill, Joe, &
what of Tom (b. 1834),
your colony boy who'll
draw into the rolling
legitimacies of their ledgers
no jot nor glyph
from serifing nibs (no matter,
mo stór, you've not been taught
to read)

term of endearment (Irish Gaelic)

***

THE BLACK NATIVES

Two of Mr. MEREDITH'S huts, and Mr. ALLEN'S have been robbed within this fortnight. Mr. DAVID RAYNER shot a black man near Mr. LYNES'S on Monday last. Nine were killed and three taken, near St. Paul's River, ten days back, and about the same time ten were shot and two taken near the Eastern Marshes. A few weeks ago, a tribe attacked Mr. MEREDITH'S horses, which had been tethered, and barbarously put two of them to death. We are daily expecting them round on the Schoutens, when all hands will be out in pursuit.

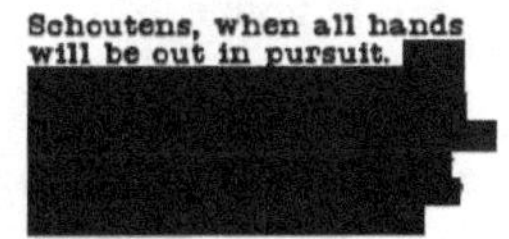

(*Colonial Times*, Friday 30 January 1829, pp. 3)

***

18.01.1830.	*Being insolent to her Mistress. Reprimanded.*
04.12.1832.	*Found drunk. 2 months. & assigned in the Interior.*
27.02.1833.	*Returned to House of Correction for assignment in the Interior.*
08.06.1833.	*Repeated drunkenness. 3 months.*
11.12.1833.	*Refusing to proceed up the country with her Mistress. Wash tub 2 months, cell at night,* hard labor, washing clothes & linen *assigned in the Interior.*
26.12.1834.	*Drunk. 1 month & assigned in the Interior.*

***

& blearily industrious, the
massacres fervid & afoot
through the deepening drear
of cottages that sink

across the sandstone terrains, lit
windows occluding the oversee
of direly Englished scenes
imagined onto the un-null &
patrolled by kingdom-white skin
that'll horror first, then
codify the unsacred
epistemically venal shift
of an unelaborated scream, o
do you hear it too, Ur-mother,
the jangle in realming heads
unasking *what to do*
if this story is yours, & **what if this story**
is yours, &
má tá an scéal seo inár dár
cad a dhéanfaidh

if this story is ours
what will we do (Irish Gaelic)

***

prisoner number 20694
free by servitude, 29th May 1835

Works Cited

"Chit Chat;" "Court Reporting;" "The Female Factory and House of Correction;" "Song." *Colonial Times*, Volume 14, Number 665, Friday 30 January 1829, pp. 3, trove.nla.gov.au/newspaper/article/8644088/666462. Accessed 04 May 2024.

[redacted] Theft (Simple Larceny) 29th May 1828." *Old Bailey Online - the Proceedings of the Old Bailey, 1674-1913 - Central Criminal Court*, www.oldbaileyonline.org/print.jsp?div=t18280529-183. Accessed 03 May 2024.

"Queens Orphanage Tasmania." *www.RootsChat.Com,* 18 July 2006, www.rootschat.com/forum/index.php?topic=170318.0. Accessed 05 May 2024.

The Literate Detective (Excerpts)

Paul Scully

Graduating to Murder

For detectives murder is febrile kisses, jagged breath, seduction. It is the most vital of crimes. It means no more daily fare of break-ins, bag snatching and fence-line feuds, return there by assignment only, with special expertise loud and lurid as you re-enter reception.

Competition for places is a ruckus: seniority, time in the queue, keeping your head high but not gun-sight lofty, merit, favouritism, inclusion criteria nowadays and deep aquifers of patience. As with becoming a detective, the petitioner must court the senior and station chief for support and prepare for multiple round-trips; mine was threefold.

Day one, posted to the outer ring of the pack, a curdling shame as I pined for a call-out–also when I practised killing thoughts–though I knew I would mostly thicken the file with routine facts, observer statements and unneighbourly suspicions, a thoroughness in default of insight.

This frisson darkened the longer I knotted an intricate death into my expectant brow but glinted occasionally with shards of sympathy and reflections on evil as the simple fatal tally mounted. In time duty, justice and the common good jostled forward. The moral compass has no feet but lengthens your stride.

My First Corpse

A ping on my skin   hail   my mind transported to my child
self   that rain could be bladed   water's benevolence
forever tainted for me   I had never known flood   Drops
now arc from my umbrella's ribs down my neck as I change
hands   the moment reasserted   Death's mercery veiling
the face   obscuring gender   a colleague cuffs my back
Ready?   I plant my foot in nervous resolve   ease into a squat
will my hand to still its tremors   A woman   an unremitting
likelihood   my breath floods my lungs   my heart buffets my sternum
a fate voided of purpose   mine now to requite   her eyes
shuttered   a sallow pallor despite the mottle of bruises

I take a full inventory of violence   cleaved lip   occluded eye
sockets   forehead abrasions   as if ploughed into a hard surface
chafed ears   a corona of blotches around the neck
hand imprints   acid scours my throat   forensics for the rest
questions that will never know a first person response

My First Solve

Through the window of the detectives' room, the sky was a sliver
on fine days, an end-stop on gloomy, the room itself a fug
of instant coffee and wildebeest armpits whatever the meteorology
or shirt print, the desktops always tussocked with unemptied ashtrays.

There were no incident rooms back then, no sticky tape or blu tack
visuals, no marker pen confabulations, just pocket notebooks we flipped
lengthwise as we decanted our measures of misbehaviour, squashed
into chairs that subverted most human shapes into question marks,

and waited for the assemblage of a melancholic or ambitious superintendent,
the one mechanical in the way of a broken-tooth typewriter, the other
prey to the logic of a gazelle, the pressure to assign blame insistent hailstones
on iron roofing whoever led the case. A first lesson emerged: look

for the forced meld when the pieces are too tongue-and-groove
or dowel perfect; the scars of a made unison are hidden from view.
(The awkwardly aligned had yet to find a light bulb in me.)
It fell to me to unpick the case chronology—a locksmith become safe

cracker—its logistical elegance such that each act and journey was deftly
tagged one to another, fore and aft, and any delay or mishap would scuttle
our suspect's alibis. As we probed the margins, our suspect resisted,
wavered, appended and revised, the thread of concoction unspooled

and he booked a saloon passage to the dock. Midnight pondering:
a half-truth punctures less easily than a bald-faced, or even bearded, lie;
past patterns frame the cross-hairs and they lock onto the obvious suspect
Occam's-razorly, indecently almost, whither our acquiescence or query?

The Days and Weeks Swell into Months and Years

Buses, trains, uniforms are sprinkled among the drowsy
when serving at transport friendly stations, detectives a dentured hen rarity,
taxis occasionally, uber aeons yet, carpooling when shifts and affability make friends,
the solo drive most common, the excuse odd hours and end time
unpredictability, but the spatial stare, a glimpse
of the void, the creative aloneness of hands on the wheel, even as the radio
might toll away the minutes and miles, these are treasures of the day not easily forsaken.
The short wave in the squad car, taken home only selectively, fizzes with static,
call-outs, orders—all argot and palsied grammar—while staccato

conversation punctures what silence remains. It is mostly shop,
the personal a rare tangent, a scudding stone, the moody trove unbreached.
When a case is closed, there is fanfare or an exasperated or treasury stalemate.
For ones where effort never flags but leads merely follow, time might
expose new morsels despite our vulturine diligence.
There are days when we juggle cyclones, others when we are marooned
in an empty freight train diverted to a desert siding spur-line or are pantomime players
in an endless season. We are prone to formulae and procedures,
and names can become like car number plates

to those not neurally dredged by vision of the corpse.
They label this survival or objectivity's necessary distance. Case-deep,
I try to consecrate a moment each day to blood-and breath-sensing the victim,
the hollowness of the erasure from the portrait on the mantlepiece,
the turn of the calendar rupturing the wound anew.
I also seek displacement in the gym, temporary by the cast
of my mind, in the pool. I have tried the bar but found it a pitfallen resort.
While my headwaters swell behind me, I am becalmed in these seething plains,
blind to the sea and the tide that will carry me there.

The Ship Lists and Sinks

Sirocco, Harmattan, this furnace wind of a dream shreds
me into wilted reeds, my wakefulness as weary as sleep.

Nightmare, daymare, it is no respecter of time, nor
the adage's healing properties.
                                        The dream has prismed

into a delta, the one person variously protagonist, character,
caricature, chimera, within and across the rivulets. The scenes

shape-shift and colour-morph at will, the narratives are involuted,
my memories mosaics.
                                Habit, instinct, discomfort in the tropics

of self ... I raided stationery for a case folder, but paused
at the title square: the cradle and flashbacks the crime scene,

the offence to raddle unrecognised images and to disquiet me,
victim, witness, abettor and sleuth? Freud, Adler and Jung

counsel that clues abound in sex, family and totems. They ransacked
the Greek myths and Latin dictionaries for labels, as if to ennoble

their theories, but they offer only fog for crime, the lives it mires,
their clotted horizons, the unredeemed purgatory of a shadowed sun.

I have taken the dream as a sign the end of my enlistment
in the penumbra is mete, I must turn the sods of another reality.

Sonnets with the Moon

Damen O'Brien

Sonnet with the Generic Moon

Eventually everybody writes a poem about the moon.
I could say orbits. I could say gravity. I could say
tides and blood and desire and you would know
I was not being honest. You would know I was being
disingenuous. Because moons are common. Ubiquitous.
Jupiter has 95 moons, Saturn has 83. Dull and dark.
When people write *moon*, they mostly mean *love*.
I could tell you that the night I saw a red moon
from a Singapore bar, all buzzed with the beer and
a sense of freedom, I thought of you in our house
far away, but that would be too convenient a truth.
I should tell you that every comet shooting across
the sky is a moon which hasn't been captured yet.

Sonnet with the Stolen Moon

My lover pulled the moon down because I asked.
Birds fall through the ragged wound that was the sky.
This gift from her hands stained with light, her guilty
smile. She gave me flowers first, a wild garland stripped
from the starlit fields. They were enough. What am I to do
with this trophy that was the moon? What am I to do
with all these frozen waves that were the heartbeat
of the Earth? What am I to do with all her love?

We went walking together in the sultry dusk
and I spoke to her of dreams and she, of fears. I hardly
heard her answers, so full of the night, her hand in mine.
That wise old moon has heard it all before.
I might have boasted of my love, even challenged hers,
but now the dawn is coming and I worry for the sun.

Sonnet with the Departing Moon

You know this story: we're losing the moon. Whatever
was said, whatever was done, it was done long ago,
in a molten moment we don't hear about, because
they're done talking and both think it best for the children
that way. No one ever asked us how we might feel,
they write silly poems that get it all wrong, they say
how nice it must be to have such a beautiful moon—
how romantic, how bright—that cold careless sphere.
But if she is to go, then let her be gone, bats cannot fly
high enough to reach her and I would not go to her
like a beggar in some rocket, like we weren't family.
She drifts further out of our orbit every year. So let that
be done. You know this story: the Earth did the best
it could for us, but every star is separate in the sky.

Sonnet with the Googled Moon

A heat map of the USA
I saw in an article shows
where Google recorded

people searching for help
for sore eyes the day
the States had its view

of a solar eclipse, a burning,
teary track passing like
Route 66, East to West.

Meant to be a joke:
hillbillies, hicks, forgot
their polarised glasses

but who wouldn't watch
the moon eat the sun?

Sonnet with the Poisoned Moon

Barn's burnt down—now I can see the moon.
—Mizuta Masahide

On Ocean Row, the windows weep. Those vulgar mansions on the wind-braced cliff, floor to ceiling showy glass, are cut with the electroplating light of the moon's long stretch across the sea and seem to weep, now that the line of eucalypts that used to bathe their stunted limbs in the salt's hard spray and obscured the view, have been pulled down by the local council workers, afraid they'd fall on some walker and her dog, there's nothing but the gulls and air between the multi-million-dollar eyes and bright-dark sea. The trees were sick, spiked with diesel herbicide, though no one knew who'd drilled their roots, a minor flap, the locals talked about for weeks and then forgot. Who would have guessed? All along, the trees had kept to themselves the moon's white rise across the bay, the roaring silver sweep of sea, that immense and glorious light. Now the mansions weep in it and on the street side of Ocean Row, windows look down on 'For Sale' signs.

Sonnet with the Watching Moon

They say if it rains under a full moon,
the moon is crying. I watched the lovers
dance on their deck, the stray cats strut,
the shine on the knife, the sheepish drunkard,
the doors slam and the doors that did not open,
a man smoking on his footstep in the quiet,
bats blink over the sky, the white waves pulse.

I watched a woman stand on a bridge
for seven nights and stare for hours while
the waters bled below, the current swift,
dark as old despair and the eighth night
when it rained, because nothing could be done,
I watched her wane and could do nothing
for I was only the weeping moon.

Sonnet with the Wrong Moon

From the Moon, the Earth is not the Moon,
phasing like faces half remembered, phrases
misunderstood, nor the Moon from the Sun, one
fleck in a forge, like forgotten words. What
absurd craters we find in our minds, unbidden
blockages, breaks in our brains, what blind
canyons, austere deserts of Alzheimer's. You said
there is a moonscape in my head, sometimes a
satellite rises, crosses the night and you are
almost alright again, but it's not the Moon, it's not
the Moon, it's the blue spite of the Earth, rising
too late, too soon. That's where all the thoughts
you wished to fly, circle, close to touch, dumb
with dust, you cover them with your thumb.

Sonnet with the Lithograph Moon

I tossed a slice of moon into a pond
and watched the koi gather at its wedge—
pared piece of radish, translucent, blond,
while radish flowers growing at the edge

dropped their purple lanterns one by one.
The moon turned, the koi turned round its face
and nudged at it until the moon was gone
or until I tossed another sliver in its place.

One koi was patchy red, one frosty white,
another, coal-black from tip to ragged tail
and the water was a cup poured full of night.
Fish scooped out of fish, scale tiled by scale

as though a tessellation, a linocut or etch of
leaves and scraps from some old artist's sketch.

Sonnet with the Swallowed Moon

The lorikeets fought over pieces of moon
on the slopes by the farmhouse with the richest soil
while in the cool shadow, we picked until noon
whatever they left us, the bowed branches full.
How does it taste to them—bickering, garrulous,
among the green leaves, white globes and blue—
this blueberry crop, silent, mysterious?
As the other moon rose, the flock of them flew,
the moon in their stomachs, our heavy yield
in a million small pieces, to raucous sounds
in valleys beyond, sewing new fields,
phasing new orbits into old ground.
We too, hauled up baskets, heavy or slight,
our mouths full of berries, filling with light.

Sonnet with the Mythic Moon

Once there were gardens on the moon,
once, goddess governed, once coyote
caught, once a wolf worried it in rabid
jaws, once a rabbit, perhaps a rabbit still,
presses its profile upon the penny light,
once man—Old Moonlight and his lantern,
once dance, once disease—shaggy disorder
howling out a madman's tune. What failed
in us? What poured through our keen
instruments? What signals bounced?
What flags persuaded us of stone
and dust? Only poets and children are
allowed to see the moon through
the telescopes of our hearts.

The snaking accuracy of cow trails

Brendan Ryan

At 7 am I'm listening to crows
reading a low-slung mountain

a line of cypresses climbing its slope.
I'm always returning as if in an endless loop

seeking attachments the Buddhists say I should
release yet my thinking is never still while walking

these paddocks more cleansing than a catholic Mass
even when the tracks are flecked with dry cow shit.

Just as there is a ritual for getting through an electrified
fence, I've snaked under bottom wires to avoid

the shock up the arm, there is a breath I've been
chasing, a way of getting the cuffs of my jeans wet.

Two ducks lift off from the river flats calling to each other
while I'm caught out by the snaking accuracy of cow trails

spreading out like arteries from a concrete trough.
Each winding trail—no more than a foot wide

descends into knee-length rye grass revealing
the path cows might take to the creek, better feed

how they read the paddocks, those flattened patches
where they have lain. I follow such mysteries

drawn by what I might have known
of dock weed and thistles. What's driving me

here is not as explainable, although the evidence
might be in the used-to-be's,

that other layer of thinking beyond feedlot farms
and shouted orders from a car window, stuff

there is no escape from yet here there are dark, cool
spaces beneath cypress plantations, memories surfacing

of cypress trees shadowing the old weatherboard.
It's this geography that buries me

as if the paddocks are embedded with cow trails
and that steep grassless hill I drove a tractor and trailer up

loaded with hay bales, front wheels of the tractor
lifting, steering lighter, giving the tractor some throttle

standing up astride the seat in case I had to jump
a trailer load of hay tipping and rolling away from me.

A Commotion of Birds

Paul Hetherington

'Many bird species and populations are under threat'
—James W Pearce

1.
We walk by the river
where jellyfish perform
murky dances in their wide tutus.
Sticky milkweed
leans into corridors
bisecting the grassland
and goats veer away.
Sweat darkens our shirts,
thrushes blink
through columns of daylight.
Pines hug shadow to the slope.

2.
A woman enters a field
and five blackbirds rise from grass,
like blown scarves
or gymnasts of the ineffable.
Two of the birds stand on air
as if there's a wire there.
A fox tiptoes up the hill
as the woman steps back,
releasing a brown falcon from a cage
in a rushing, unkempt dance.

3.
Egrets stand—seven of them
like apostles of the estuary.

(Your father pointed them out
when you could barely walk
and every year since
you've seen their faces change,
as if adopting the forest's tones.)
He beckons you to return
where he fishes
as you imagine flying
over the water's
shining exclamation
until you're all motion,
your face greening,
nuptial plumes
caressing your back.

4.
An estuary narrows
to a brackish ribbon, meandering
through encrusted sand
to a granulated trickle
where waders gather.
Tender laterite hues
paint the water
in undulant violet
and shivering blue-silver.
Birds and insects
are tessellations of light.

5.
Through square-seeming minutes
awkward notions swoop and lift,
leaving swathes of broken colour.
Afternoons of failing sunlight
contain words we didn't say
in time, when failure closed our hands.

‘Tomorrow’, you insist,
as if the word hinges everything.
As the river floods, carrying a year’s detritus—
branches, bicycles and an old car seat—
parrots fly from the fruit trees.

6.
Thousands of starlings
circle the city
in swirls of grey,
as if escaping a deluge.
Their screaming
is an expostulation, heard
through cracked, tilted glass.

7.
In the difficult days there was always
the memory of the raven we’d gathered
from turbulent sleet—fragile, nearly naked
in its broken feathers,
that over seven weeks
we fed and revived.

You released it one morning, walking near
the wood pile, warmth pricking air
like thousands of beakings, as spring pressed
tense coils of growth—
you extended your arm
to the scurrying wind.

Afterwards, it was a feathery glint
amid conversation, and I thought of it
like an important word—
a noun holding fast
despite the ragged edges
of too much speech.

Notes on the Dragon year

Jane Skelton

1

the creek unfurls its dragon tongue
                                        copper-coloured rage

here it comes

  hear the hiss

Charybdis   licking up
depth marker sign flood zone sign dead tyres
  a rollicking fairground ride
    spit-frothed

the bridge snaps easy   we watch it pass

mesmeric, it summons you
                                    meet locals never seen before

even dogs subdued

we can only stare at this soup-swell
eyes flick to each other
  and back to the wave-drunk
                                      creek-now-river

at our feet the suck and reek, sludge and humic mat

here it comes

through earth's pores, it pulses cold
                                          up legs, spines
into blood, and beats—shocking skulls

step back, further back!
in flood's knife glint
                                    past selves unravel
memories trace the creek's old path
stranded ghosts in sepia tide

2
how it was?
  a trickle, clear honey chain of pools
water dragons, stone-coloured
     clung above the garrulous falls

tea-tree, myrtle, bowed low
  pollens dusting its face
clouds slept in pools
     rocks floated on sky

dragonfly traced yin-yang
  wings of paper light
paused as though listening—
     then, the red baron dart

goanna, of dot-patterned armour
  flexed claws, licked air with forked tongue
scraped belly over doily-draped rock
     yawned, moved on

mirror through to grainy sand
  green streak of river weed
in breathing water, galaxias swarmed
     we slapped march flies, fed to fry

men fished for eel in tannin pools
  caught a leech or two
red leg dribble
     red toe bloom

I stepped through the riffle
  the chuckling zone
cobbles played
  by fizzy water
my outline fragmented, shirred
    shrank, ballooned

and time disappeared

how it was?
  in blue day's click and chirr
summer's palpitating heart
pricked, shivered—water and skin
    you, upon a lichen rock, hair haloed by sun

3
here it comes comes again
not only tipsy but drunken
swaying across the grass—
rain addicted to earth
anxious stutter across a map
primary colours converging
red-centred tail thrash
seeking, sliding, a confluence
of tongues
from drone's eye view
this yellow stuff, this gelbstoff
ochreous, gilded in sun's hard glitter
a mirrorland
looks solid, walkable
a suburban phantasmagoria
a J.G. Ballard dream

the motionless orderly lines of rooftops
treetops powerlines, empty canals of streets

the flooded land seems tranquil, tamed
calmed by all it has gathered
logshousespeoplecarstreesscrubanimalsmetal

but hear the low tenor sigh
an undercurrent seething
seething
hear the water's secret desire

4

as water weaves and runs
beneath the drifting town
we watch through mouldy lace
our maculated veil
nature devouring nature
each element taking its turn

I part the curtains
and see at water's fringe—
spearheads of striated ripples
here they come
swivelling up the hill
heads raised and eyes intent
water dragons crouch, green-flushed
crested heads crane up
caper forward   freeze
   caper forward   freeze
as one

claws scrabble iron—
dragons take over the roof-top
congregate, as waters rise
guarding deities or gargoyles
   contemplate the drowning eye

5

cast a line and watch it arc into violet air
fishing through the mud days
in the mud taint
where tardigrades tumble, unconcerned
the return of dogs people boats
houses plucked from log jams, log jams disassembled
the drowned exhausted town behind me
the murmur of trucks and cranes and tinnies' snarl
and cockcrows from rooftops
the dainty tugging a tender picking
a plec on a string
soft mouths of tiddlers and crabs' claws teasing
an invisible tearing
I reel in my desiccated Thailand prawn
line weed-strung dribbling over the muddy bank
clouds broil and lather up
  we wait
tears and blood pulsing the tidal beat

6

even if I tell you how it was
in Kodachrome memories fading, curling

I'm of the Great Forgetting

the present etches the future line
the past in the layers

the strata, in books of mud
smudged black detritus
        the wall's flood streak
scorched forests and midden shells disgorged

we *can* find the familiar in wild eyes
in the eyes of fishes

even reptiles
a companionship of sorts, an alliance

when we think of how it was
we are shimmering
in the cleansing water of eyelids

and yet there may be only this—
arm around and strong hand grip
holding on
for the fast ride

Grass Sonnets

Jennifer Harrison

Grass

Ragged, unkempt, sprawling beside
a roadside, growing wild in the smoky air,
weed grass inhabits the space
between concrete culvert and bush.
The way genealogy is peripheralised
but sucks obstinately at the sun.
Shifting direction now, wind ruffling
the glint in grass, like hair, which
now you think is a metaphor for something
skullish that lives like a stone goblin
beneath family appearances … no …
nothing bald or buried like a rock …
more a hibernation, folklore, or talisman,
the undead smirking at us from the earth.

Earth

Every family has their particular secrets.
In yours, they were questions:
why did your father's mother bear eleven
(maybe twelve) children to someone
she didn't really like? Why was your
mother's mother abandoned as a child
to be raised by a Marni (which became
the only word for nurture in the family)?
Today, time falls in swathes of burning
letters to make way for an overgrown
path that leads through old grass, the dry
fields shimmering. Tomorrow, you say,
will be a good day when you find stillness
or, maybe, when waiting feels like silence.

Silence

A bell distantly shrills. You hear
its echo slither from an old school belfry,
a tinnitus that's meant to call down
the purest of clarion gods from sky's
classroom somewhere above the clouds.
Peal. The word brittle. Bright. An *ism*
truncated like an imprecation to the
lost prayer of meaning. For some reason
you think of pipes coming and going,
taking away what we don't need,
bringing back clean water and ducted
air. And now you hear cicadas singing,
Green Grocers and Black Princes,
their cellophane wings, wet and blue-lit.

Blue-lit

Snaking veins return oxygen's dusk
to the heart. Above winter mountains:
the icy sky. This chair is covered with
azure wool and your grandson watches
his favourite Bluey reruns on TV.
In her cotton dress mother did the laundry
(father loving how the fabric matched
exactly the colour of her eyes). In the
Whirlpool she placed a small square
package of meshed blue dye that seeped
slowly through the wash like night salts
leaching into the ocean. A mood. Kiama
blowhole subsiding back into a headland's
erosion. No waste. In one colour, all colours.

Colours

A rainbow hangs in a corner
of the rinsed sky, its spectrum of light
an arched palate crying out to the retina
like a song—it's what you glimpsed
and still see as the car angles around
J-corners and slides into the future's
messy mirage. Unrooted. Permanent
transience. A phenomenon through
which to view the past with clearer
jouissance, memory like a soldier crab
burying instinct in mounds of crumbed
sand, where you walk sideways, almost
furtively, careful not to touch the shadows
that throw cracks irregularly on the path.

Path

You'd prefer to do without the word
'like' but haven't figured out linkage
yet—how to make sense of 'here' versus
'there' and fully understand the best
words for 'otherness': the 'self' a construction
hovering in peripheries of environment
where scrub has been cleared away to
make a nest for houses, offices, roads, cars.
Luggage. Electricity. You remember
how the BMW flew along a country road,
the wind like a creature tearing at your vizor
(it always took two days to untangle
your hair)—and, even then, you knew
how to lose your way, lose a destination.

Destination

You want to understand whether
a poem needs more specificity,
more riddles collaged from puzzles
that seem philosophical only to chance.
It's about the pedestrian outside your
house this morning who said 'excuse me'
as he stepped aside to let you pass,
or maybe he barged right on, unseeing,
preoccupied with the person he might
be meeting up ahead, that place being
not so much a 'destination' as grass
growing from the centre of a pond,
pushing whimsy against the wind, an image
if not yet in another's, specific in your mind.

Mind

The Pizza Hut fired you for coming
late to the 'Submarine' workshop high
with a friend, and then refusing to sing
to the patrons when bringing out
their birthday ice-cream cake. You
knew the manager liked you anyway
(he rehired you two more times after that)
but you were tone deaf and couldn't hold
a job. Nobody. *Not him or anyone else owns*
anyone else, you thought, naïve, but likeable.
A leader, you were plunging head-first
into a tub of toffee apples, crocodile teeth
snapping, but like all adages summarised,
almost missed your own suburban story.

Story

Watching Season 4 of *Blown Away*
on Netflix, you suspect you have nothing
much to write about and so fish the ether
for television, sand and hard air—
natron, flux, borosilicate and scar-flame—
how the assistants clip off the bottom
of a hot sculpture, sometimes a dome or vase
shattering across the floor into lacerated
pieces or imploding in the annealer—
except *they* have only one go at making
their art perfect which is now
what you try to do: editing nothing out,
allowing the poem to crash until you, too,
are used to losing what's lovingly made.

Made

He introduced himself as a woodsman,
a furniture craftsman who'd worked
all his artisanal life to create installations,
bespoke pieces that, like bush country,
would bear the marks of cinder sticks
burned into chairs, tables and cabinets.
At our house, his sons carry
a hardwood bookshelf down the hall
and later we sit together in the sun
making memories of a meal, sweat
and laughter. *Choosing the right part*
of a fallen tree is easy, he says, sons nodding,
while another friend draws trees on paper,
in pencil, until a leaf has grown on one.

Hyaena song

Kathryn Lomer

The hyaenas are calling her backwards and forwards
to her home or her future. She has no home:
their *tukul* holds only the ghost of a sneer,
the washbowl and rags of her shame.
                    Her husband slept
on their goatskin bed
and she tried to be quiet
as the moon in her belly struggled.
Lightning jagged in her body;
a storm ripped from her north to her south
bringing, as ever, no rain, no ease,
hours turning to stanzas of pain.
          Something has eaten her flesh;
she is buried alive in a darkness which hurts
with the weight of the earth; the world is crushing
her bones. She is learning to whisper the song
hyaenas howl as she crosses their land.
                              The first bird she meets
is a bearded vulture, its knowledge
in wing, beak and claw,
hers in the pelvis and soles of her feet.
Come play me the *krar*, she cries,
so your music can help me walk,
but minstrels are just like the others.
          Now the hyaena's call
splits into syllables; they converse
with ululations of oceans;
of course she has never seen one.
Birds fly over her, bright bolts of cloth
new from the market. Her arms feel the gravity
of this world. She's been told the earth
is crossed with lines, like a child's game

scratched with a twig in the dust,
so everyone knows where they are.
                    Still she is lost.
Those unmoving mountains stick in her throat;
no water to wash them down or out;
they are stencilled onto the backs of her eyes.
Each fiery dusk and moody dawn is drawn
over her like stitches or patches of quilt;
she is suffocating; how can she breathe?
      This land
littered with famine bones
is larger than she could have known,
never imagining she could feel so alone.
How many people are there? she wonders.
Glyphs in the sand may be telling the answer
but she's never learned to read.
She tended their cows and vegetables,
cooked over dung,
hoped to give birth to a son.
                    She is being called
into emptiness; it sucks
at her fingers and toes. The dust
of this land fills up her lungs.
The sun crosses above her so many times
that part of her travels with it. She knows
the earth she is walking walks too,
swims or spins on its axis in space;
if she stands still in the heat she can feel it.
                    In Lalibela
there are churches hewn from the rock;
she will petrify with this heat and heaviness;
unearthed, engraved, her body turned temple
where people pray for souls of the lost,
her open thighs will welcome them into pain.
Unholy thoughts will be entombed forever in stone:
Christos, where were you?

She looks heavenward
for comfort, but finds respite
in a tree lizard's eye. Colour
is subtracted from another day;
she moves through monotone seeing creatures
stranger than in her grandmother's fire stories.
At the edge of one village
a man greets her *Tadiyass!*, swings her up on his back.
His hip bones cut into her thighs and she smells
her smell on him. Will he take up a stone,
knock her on the head, take a knife to her throat
like a goat on a saint's day? Can this be God's will?
She has no fear for this life when he sets her down,
but when he kisses her torn feet something rises
inside her the way they say water swells
in empty wells when it rains far away.
Slow and steady. She is the well
and the water which runs down her cheeks
and her thighs; the dust in her eyes washes away.
Lions sing
the power of good deeds, the might
of small things, and for seven days
those kisses banish the pain of each step.
He had parchment skin and ceremonial eyes
like a priest.
The *wogesha* told her
it was preordained her baby should die,
so why was her body punished?
I will be my own priest, she thinks,
and *wogesha*, and lion, and hyaena.
The striped hyaena eats bones and teeth;
will my spirit be his? Will his be mine?
I will lay him a bowl of porridge to know my end.
Hunger
is her normal state but this is new—
a thinning of skull, flesh made dust.

She has seen pots and plates crumble;
she's made of the same local earth.
She walks into the rainy season,
dissolving. Help me, she cries, I am clay.
          Five days
to give stillbirth, unconscious for three,
it is only now, hours from Addis Ababa,
that she gives her lost daughter a name—Tesfaye,
my hope—and dedicates her tears.
                                        The doctors say
to rest for the operation,
give her water, some *tef*, a bed.
She tells them her wedding-bread name is Desta,
which means pleasure.
          Princess Tsehai hospital becomes home:
to welcome other women, Desta lays a table
on freshly cut grass, scoops
a handful of coffee beans for the mortar
and slams in the pestle with the rhythm of walking.

About The Poets

Claire Albrecht

Claire Albrecht is an award-winning poet and editor based on Wiradjuri Country. Her work investigates connections between mental health, the physical environment, and technology. Claire's poem 'The Anabranch' won the 2022 Newcastle Poetry Prize, and her work has featured in Best of Australian Poems anthologies.

Emilie Collyer

Emilie Collyer writes poetry, plays and prose. Her poetry collection *Do you have anything less domestic?* (Vagabond Press, 2022) won the inaugural Five Islands Press Prize and she was runner up in the 2024 Gwen Harwood Poetry Prize. She is currently an Adjunct Industry Fellow at RMI.

B. R. Dionysius

B. R. Dionysius was founding Director of the Queensland Poetry Festival. He has published nine collections of poetry. His latest collection, *Critical State* was published in 2022. He teaches English & Literature & watches birds. His tenth collection, *The Eromanga Sea* and his eleventh collection, *Extinction Sonnets* are forthcoming in 2025.

Dan Disney

Dan Disney is based in Seoul, where he is a tenured professor with Sogang University's English Literature program. His latest publication is *Thuggery, Buggery, Skullduggery Inc.* (Red Letter Press, 2024).

Jo Gardiner

Recently, Jo Gardiner was a finalist in the Montreal International Poetry Prize, the Newcastle Poetry Prize, and the University of Canberra Vice Chancellor's International Poetry Prize. Her novel, *The Concerto Inn* (UWA Publishing), appeared in 2006. Her poetry collection, *The Impossible Shore*, is forthcoming from Vagabond Press in 2024.

Elena Gomez

Elena Gomez lives on unceded Wurundjeri country. She is the author of *Body of Work* and *Admit the Joyous Passion of Revolt* along with several chapbooks and pamphlets.

Jennifer Harrison

Jennifer Harrison has written eight books of poetry, most recently *Anywhy* (Black Pepper 2018). Three new collections *Sideshow History, Fowler's Phrenology* and *Finals* are forthcoming in 2024/2025. She is Chair of the World Psychiatry Association's Section for Art and Psychiatry and won the 2023 Troubadour International Poetry Prize.

Paul Hetherington

Paul Hetherington has published 18 full-length collections of poetry, including *Sleeplessness*, which won the inaugural The Marion Halligan Award in 2024. He founded International Poetry Studies at the University of Canberra and the international Prose Poetry Project. With Cassandra Atherton he co-authored *Prose Poetry: An Introduction* (Princeton University Press, 2020).

A. Frances Johnson

A. Frances Johnson is an award-winning writer, artist and recovering academic. Her most recent poetry collection is *Save As* (Puncher and Wattmann, 2021). She has published four collections of poetry, a novel *Eugene's Falls* (Arcadia, 2007) and a monograph, *Australian Fiction as Archival Salvage* (Brill, 2015). In 2020, she won the International ABR Peter Porter Poetry Prize.

Christopher (Kit) Kelen

Published widely since the seventies, Christopher (Kit) Kelen has more than a dozen full length collections in English as well as translated books of poetry in a dozen languages other than English. Kit's latest volume of poetry in English is *Book of Mother*, published by Puncher & Wattmann in 2022.

Jennifer Kornberger

Jennifer Kornberger is a writer and artist who employs poetry as a primary practice for public art works, installations and publication. Her poetry has appeared in major journals including *Blue Dog, Plumwood Mountain*, and the Newcastle Poetry Prize anthology. A full-length collection, *I could be rain*, was published by Sunline Press. Installation works include '22 Pillars' and 'Somnus', both commissioned by The Fremantle Biennale.

Shari Kocher
Shari Kocher is an Australian poet, fiction-writer, educator and therapist. She holds a PhD in Creative Writing from Melbourne University and is the author of two poetry collections published by Puncher & Wattmann: *The Non-Sequitur of Snow* (2015) and *Foxstruck and Other Collisions* (2021). The former title was shortlisted for the FAW Anne Elder Award (2015) and the latter was Highly Commended at the NSW Premier's Literature Awards in the Kenneth Slessor Poetry Prize (2022). *www.sharikocher.com*

Verity Laughton
(Dr) Verity Laughton is an award-winning playwright and poet. Her more than 30 works have been produced in Australia, New Zealand, Korea, Japan, the UK and the USA. Her most recent production is the sell-out adaptation of Pip Williams' novel, *The Dictionary of Lost Words*.

Kathryn Lomer
Kathryn Lomer has published eight books with University of Queensland Press, across the genres of poetry, fiction, short fiction and young adult fiction. Her most recent poetry collection, *Afterlife*, was published by Puncher and Wattmann in 2023.

J. Marahuyo
J. Marahuyo is a neurodivergent Filipino-Australian award winning poet. Her debut *4:37am; crying gorgeously* will be published early 2025 by WestWords Books. Her work is in *Cordite Poetry Review*, and *FemAsia*. When she's not writing she is pspsp-ing cats, or getting on the wrong train. Her instagram is @j_marahuyo

Mal McKimmie
Mal McKimmie is the author of four poetry collections, the most recent being *The Diwan of Nawid* (Puncher & Wattmann, 2024) and *At the Foot of the Mountain* (Puncher & Wattmann, 2021). *The Brokenness Sonnets I-III & Other Poems* (Five Islands, 2011), was the 2012 Age Poetry Book of the Year.

Greg McLaren
Greg McLaren is a poet living on Darug Country in the NSW Blue Mountains. He is the author of the dystopian verse novel *camping underground*. Other books include *The Kurri Kurri Book of the Dead, Australian ravens* and *Windfall* (all Puncher & Wattmann).

Glenn McPherson

Glenn McPherson is a Sydney based poet. He has been widely published in leading Journals and Anthologies. Recent poems can be found in *Modern Haiku, Catchment* and *InDaily*.

Andrew Menken

Andrew is currently doing a PhD at the University of Newcastle. Many of his lyrics are imaginative explorations of his small coastal hometown of Budgewoi. Andrew's poetry has appeared in *Westerly, Quadrant, The Suburban Review, SWAMP* and *Cordite*. In 2021, he received the Allen and Unwin Award for Creative Writing.

Scott-Patrick Mitchell

Scott-Patrick Mitchell received the 2022 Red Room Poetry Fellowship, the 2023 XYZ Prize and was Highly Commended in the 2024 Blake Poetry Prize. Their debut poetry collection *Clean* (Upswell Publishing, 2022) was shortlisted for The Prime Minister's Literary Awards, The WA Premier's Book Awards and The Victorian Premier's Literary Awards.

Damen O'Brien

Damen O'Brien is a multi-award-winning poet based in Brisbane. His prizes include The Moth Poetry Prize and the Newcastle Poetry Prize. His poems have been published in seven countries, nominated for a Pushcart Prize and highly commended in the Forward Prize. Damen's latest book is *Walking the Boundary*.

Verity Oswin

Verity Oswin is a prize-winning poet, documentary producer and mother undertaking her doctorate in Creative Writing at the University of Adelaide. Her feminist pastoral poetry explores the poetics of empire and settler relationships to the land.

Jenny Pollak

Jenny Pollak is an artist and poet. Her work has appeared in various journals and anthologies, including *Meanjin; Cordite; the Australian Poetry Journal; Red Room Poetry, Verity La*, and *Australian Award Winning Writing*. Her first collection of poetry, *Clarion*, was published this year by Liquid Amber Press.

Sarah Rice

Sarah Rice's first poetry collection *Fingertip of the Tongue* won the Eyelands International Book Awards. Sarah won the Ron Pretty, the Bruce Dawe, and co-won the Writing Ventures, and Gwen Harwood poetry prizes, and has been shortlisted in numerous national and international writing awards. Her work has been published extensively.

Brendan Ryan

Brendan Ryan lives in Geelong, his most recent book of poetry is *Feldspar* (Recent Work Press, 2023). His New and Selected poems will be published in 2025.

Paul Scully

Paul Scully is a Sydney-based poet with three published collections, the latest being *The Fickle Pendulum* by Interactive Press in 2021. His poems have been commended and shortlisted in major Australian prizes and published in print and online journals in Australia, Ireland, the UK and USA. His website is *www.paulscullypoet.com.au*

Nathan Shepherdson

Nathan Shepherdson is the author of ten books of poetry. His most recent titles are *soft meteorites* (Upswell), *axolotl waltz* (Puncher & Wattmann), and *parallel equators* (Recent Work Press). He is an occasional essayist and sometime collaborator with other artists. He was born and lives in Meanjin/Brisbane.

Jane Skelton

Jane Skelton lives in the Blue Mountains on Dharug land. She is widely published in magazines and anthologies. Her poetry collection *What the River Told Me* was published by Flying Islands. It followed *Chimera*, (prose and poetry), *Lives of the Dead and Other Stories* and *Flying Foxes* (a novella).

David Stavanger

David Stavanger is a poet, producer, parent, and lapsed psychologist living on Dharawal land. Co-editor of *Admissions: Voices Within Mental Health* (Upswell, 2022), David's last collection *Case Notes* (UWAP, 2020) won the 2021 Victorian Premier's Literary Award for Poetry. This poem will be in his next book, *The Drop Off* (Upswell, 2025).

Mark Tredinnick

Mark Tredinnick is a celebrated Australian poet whose honours include two Newcastle Poetry Prizes, the Montreal and the Blake. *A Beginner's Guide, House of Thieves,* and *Nine Carols* are his most recent books. Mark is the editor of *Bright Crockery Days* (5Islands, 2024), a volume of essays in celebration of Robert Gray.

www.ingramcontent.com/pod-product-compliance
Lightning Source LLC
Chambersburg PA
CBHW030635120726
47904CB00006B/2164

* 9 7 8 0 6 4 5 3 7 5 6 6 4 *